Moderate to Poor, Occasionally Good

Moderate to Poor, Occasionally Good

Eley Williams

4th ESTATE • *London*

4th Estate
An imprint of HarperCollins*Publishers*
1 London Bridge Street
London SE1 9GF

www.4thestate.co.uk

HarperCollins*Publishers*
Macken House, 39/40 Mayor Street Upper
Dublin 1, D01 C9W8, Ireland

First published in Great Britain in 2024 by 4th Estate

1

Copyright © Eley Williams 2024

Eley Williams asserts the moral right to be identified
as the author of this work in accordance with the
Copyright, Designs and Patents Act 1988

A catalogue record for this book is
available from the British Library

ISBN 978-0-00-861892-6 (hardback)
ISBN 978-0-00-861893-3 (trade paperback)

Set in Stempel Garamond LT Std
Printed and bound in the UK using 100%
renewable electricity at CPI Group (UK) Ltd

for A & A, forever

Contents

Scrimshaw

Not knowing what else to do, I send you walruses.

It's an online feed maintained by the Alaska Department of Fish & Game with cameras trained on a state sanctuary twenty-four hours a day, seven days a week. The caption claims that what you're looking at is one of the largest gathering places in the world for Pacific walruses. If the season's right, you can watch 15,000 walruses rolling about and sunning themselves: puffy and hairy and taking stock of their walrus days. It's a go-to site for me, bookmarked and ready for whenever insomnia has me in its jaws. There is audio too: one cursor nudge and your speakers thrum with huffing and wuffing, moustachioed blurts and bluster-ings of never-footed scuffling all in real time.

By this point we had been messaging for hours, my face close to the phone screen, imagining you doing the same. A whole town stretched between us, and it was something of a comfort to consider the surface of our separate skins blued or bluewn or bluesed by the same pixel-light, typing against our own private darknesses.

We had dispatched small talk, sweet talk, sweet nothings and then came your message stating that you were feeling unhappy.

We're all feeling unhappy, I thought. Would that be a helpful thing to say? I meant it with solidarity but perhaps it would read as dismissive. Flushed with responsibility for your state of mind I flexed my thumbs, considering my options. I couldn't ask you about your day because perhaps it was the cause of your unhappiness and making you dwell on it would simply compound the problem. I couldn't tell you about *my* day because that certainly was the cause of *my* unhappiness, and now wasn't the time to be competitive. I couldn't comment on the weather, or the politics, the price of either and neither of those things because it all led to the same thing: unhappiness *unhappiness* unhappiness.

I typed the first letter of possible responses to you, playing for time. I thought about the corresponding three rippling dots on your phone screen and read your message again.

The word *unhappy* implies something of a void. A state of *not-happiness*, sure, but not necessarily anyone actively gasping in despair. I twitched my thumb away from our conversation to check an online thesaurus. *Cheerlessness, desolation, despair, despondency, dolefulness, downheartedness, gloom, gloominess, glumness, malaise, wretchedness*: I could ask you which one might be the most appropriate, listing them in alphabetical order so as not to imply my own personal hierarchy in terms of the terms.

I returned to your message none the wiser but making sure I typed something in the field so that three dots would show I was keeping you company. You didn't know I was stalling rather than composing. Those dots change in character depending on one's mood: the same ellipsis could just as easily signal a drumroll of anticipation, a trail of Hansel and Gretel breadcrumbs leading you on, or the side of a rolled dice when your guess is as good as mine. I dithered and felt the pressure of the dots out there shifting, undulating, modulating the shade of the blue light on your face as you waited for a message to materialise.

I drafted a breath then deleted it.

You cannot be in control of another person's feelings is a phrase I once overheard. As I recall I was on a bus and a mother was saying it to her daughter, but I suppose it could just have easily been a therapist taking her client on a trip. Not a bad idea, all things considered: bagsy a top-deck seat first thing in the morning then spend the day travelling up and down the bus route, letting a series of your analysands unburden themselves one by one as you criss-cross the city. Cheaper than renting an office; moquette seat-covers right there as free Rorschach tests; all the *alight*, *baggage*, *journey* metaphors right there for the taking. I saved this eavesdropped phrase to the Notes app on my phone as soon as I heard it and emboldened the words just to make it stick.

I don't want you to be unhappy. I don't want you to dwell on it. I don't want you to dwell on the fact I only want to dwell on you. *Undwell, antidwell, disdwell.* I wanted you to think me breezy, authoritative, admirable, so maybe it would be best not to acknowledge what you had said at all and breezily, authoritatively, admirably re-direct your attention. Diversion as care.

You cannot be in control of another person's feelings.

I copy–paste the link to the walrus live-stream and send it your way.

Walruses belong to that subset of animals that are twee but also somehow noble in their anatomical absurdity. They look like they were designed for the purposes of an Edward Lear poem. SEE ALSO: penguins, pelicans, flamingos, koalas. I could list those to you in alphabetical order to avoid implying a hierarchy of preference: *flamingos, koalas, pelicans, penguins, walruses.* Walruses look frustrated and benign On some level, I must have thought that this might be an appropriate response to your unhappiness: I am sorry for frustrations; you were right to tell me; I can be your technique for distraction.

You have not replied.

I draw my phone closer to my face and flick through to another app. I read facts about walruses in case my link acted as an opener for further conversation between us. If so, I'll be ready. The family name for walruses is *Odobenidae.* Maybe that's one of those words that has the same shape as its meaning. Another one of these words is *bed.* You can see what I mean in lowercase: bed. You can see the headboard and the footrest and a little plumping of duvet there. Maybe *llama* is another one: the shape of the word looks like a llama sitting down, its legs tucked beneath its body. Just so, *Odobenidae* is a walrus lying, merman aslant, on its side. I consider typing all this to you but want to make sure you have responded to the link first. Maybe it will take a while for you to work out what I've sent you. Perhaps your connection is poor. I thumb through more facts.

I can distract you, I draft. I delete. *I want to drive you to distraction*, I try typing. No. Dot dot dot. *I love*

5

you, I draft in my text message, a word for each dot drip-drip water-torturing your phone's screen. I delete the draft. On idling instinct and left on Read, I click the link that I sent you to the walrus colony. The page begins to load: *REFRESHING STREAM* it reads. Soon, I think: a simplicity of walruses in a refreshing stream.

Nobody seems to have a clear idea of the etymology of the word *walrus*. I skip along already-open tabs on my phone. 'A variety of walrus found in the North Pacific has sometimes received the distinct specific name *obesus*.' I roll in my bed and chew the cud of that fact. *You cannot be in control of another person's feelings.* Another site claims that a name given to the ivory of their tusks is *morse*. The page shows small objects, crucifixes and jewellery made from sawn tuskbone. I keep clicking links, not taking anything in as I wait for a notification from you. Pages and pages all about walruses, cryptic and coded in their fat-headedness, *Odobenidae* morsey and moreish. My phone becomes a rogues' gallery montage of silly walrus faces standing up on wealthy white stilts; reams of them, herds of them; infinite walrus.

I throw my phone across the bed and wait until the screen turns black before I scoop it up again and cradle its re-brightened screen by my head.

You have not replied. It has been minutes. Usually you are quicker than this. My phone tells me it's 4:02, which doesn't look like the shape of anything. I check to see what is happening on the live-feed of walruses and I'm relieved to see that the page has finally loaded. I would not have wanted to send you a dead link, sent you down a dead-end.

The walruses on my screen are grey and pink. They look like they are brawling. I pinch and zoom, click to hear the audio. No, not brawling. The walruses are roaring as they not-brawl.

I realise I have sent you a link to a live-stream of thousands of walruses mating. It is obscenely in high definition, as obscene and absurd and violent and loafish as 4:02 on a clock face and I have never been more awake in my life.

The walruses mate on as I draft a thousand different apologies, a horrified array of horrified pre-programmed reactions – face-draining emoji, Edvard Munch scream emoji, uppercase letter D colon emoticon – but none are quite right so I draft and delete and I wait and wait and I am so unhappy, *dejected*, wretched. There are no three dots from you in answer, not even the beginning of an SOS because you have fallen asleep? Switched your phone off? Ceased to exist entirely, drafted and deleted and done with it all? I concentrate on ceasing to exist, on the fact *you cannot be in control of another person's feelings* having once been good advice, but all I know now is that there's a blue glow between my fingers and I am fully awake, and all around me and once around you is some kind of braying and something like lancing, remorseful, loud and long and clear.

Wilgefortis

There was a certain amount of gentleness in the way the other girls pushed the locker door shut on her, as if careful not to get their fingers or hair caught in the hinges. Jenny began praying once she heard their footsteps recede down the corridor, and she had a new saint ready to go, but suddenly in the act of petition she second-guessed her pronunciation of the chosen saint's name. She had only ever seen it written down. She really hoped that she hadn't completely ballsed up getting her prayer answered on that basis. Jenny did not usually pray out loud but today, now, crouching in the dark of the slammed sports locker, it seemed important that she should *declare* the words rolling around her head rather than merely think them. After all, *saying* something *fervently* surely counted for more or far more than *thinking* something fervently. Maybe twice as much. It would give the prayer more staying power, as if the breath and effort of speech would propel the prayer that crucial inch higher to the heavens, and increase the chance of attracting the saint's attention.

She had read the name in so many captions, scrolled through what felt like hundreds of articles and forum posts all about their life and performed miracles, but never once during all that had Jenny questioned the way the name should sound when spoken out loud. Jenny really didn't want to waste the saint's time or, worse, undermine any petition by stumbling on their name straight off the bat. She had not been raised in a family that had much time for religion and was not entirely clear on the mechanics of how prayer might work – couldn't say whether it was more like making a wish than hailing a cab. The right pronunciation was the least she could do, though, surely. She didn't want her petition to be misdirected into the void or whatever, just because it hadn't been addressed in the right way. It might ping back, embarrassingly, resolutely undelivered, marked RETURN TO SENDER.

Jenny trialled her best guess, her breath warming the sheet metal door in front of her nose.

Wil-guh-fortis, hear my prayer.

That had a good bounce and spring to it, Jenny thought, and seemed likely to fit better scansion-wise into the lines of hymns than any alternative. That's as good an indicator as any, Jenny thought, and she said the name again into the close air of the locker, and instantly the word took on the taste of her surroundings, a concentration of the changing rooms where she had been locked: sweat; old, dried mud on shin guards; the root-beer-sweet stink of school-regulation plimsolls.

Wilgefortis, hear my prayer. The door of the metal locker was thin and the cloakroom window was open; whoops of the other girls in the sports field outside drifted occasionally overhead as they played hockey or netball or some other pivoting game.

Jenny was praying for clarity, for strength in her convictions. She decided to decide: *Wil-guh-fortis.* She told herself that if she sounded out the name with the best intentions in her heart, there would be no harm.

On the bus ride on her way home, Jenny read that St Wilgefortis is also occasionally known as 'Uncumber'. In Holland, she's called 'Ontkommer' too. Google Translate implied that the word *ontkommer* roughly approximates to *escaper*. In France, Wilgefortis is known as 'Débarras'. This translates as *riddance*.

At times of stress, Jenny had developed a habit of pressing a finger into that natural depression between her nose and her upper lip. Once she learned that there was a word for this depression, she found she was forever repeating it in her head – *philtrum philtrum philtrum* from the Greek, literally meaning *love charm*. What is the point in school if it's all on our phones, she thought, as the bus pulled up by her home.

Many people know about the word *philtrum*. Many people claim it as their favourite word. You may have heard of St Wilgefortis because she is depicted in religious art and iconography as sporting a thick, lustrous beard.

Thinking about favourite saints, and beards, and words, Jenny locked the bathroom door behind her.

'You shouldn't listen to what Vanessa says,' her best friend Anna had told her earlier that afternoon as they stood in the queue for lunch.

'But do I? Do I have one?' Jenny had asked. She did not like seeing her friend try to lie so as she spoke she kept her eyes fixed on the school canteen's fridges. The only remaining sandwiches were tuna and cucumber. The very worst of the worst of the worst. After four years at school, Jenny had trained herself to recognise tuna and cucumber sandwiches from the furthest limits of the queue by the little blue cartoon fish on the corner of the packaging. The cartoon fish gave Jenny the thumbs up, illustrating that the tuna was dolphin-friendly.

'You can only really see it when you stand in profile,' Anna replied.

'But I'm always standing in profile for somebody.'

'It's just downy, Jenny. Don't worry about it.'

It's just downy. It's just puppy fat. You are somewhere between a duckling and a young dog, Jenny. Don't worry about it.

Jenny put down her tray, walked from the lunch hall and went out into the rain to the bus stop. The word *downy downy downy downy* played in her ears all the way home, knelling in a new headache for her. She placed her finger on her upper lip and prayed to St Wilgefortis. *Philtrum philtrum philtrum.*

There have been sculptures and carvings of St Wilgefortis dating from the eleventh century. She resembles the familiar crucified Christ in the iconography – narrow-faced and looking down with pained benevolence from the cross. Long hair with a centre parting and a beard reaching the chest. The full-length flowing tunic is the giveaway. In later paintings of St Wilgefortis, this is a beautiful, embroidered dress covered in flowers, and she wears soft blue slippers.

Jenny switched on the bathroom light and watched all the surfaces come back bright and brash at her. It took one blink – one breath, four steps and a single semi-slip in her socks to get to the medicine cabinet. As she pulled its mirror-fronted doors open, Jenny watched her reflection halve itself straight down the middle. The cabinet was overstuffed and some plasters and an emery board fell into the sink straight from the shelves. She picked them back up and lined them according to size next to her mother's special menthol toothpaste. She put the emery board beneath them as an underline as if for emphasis. Jenny began searching the cabinet. She flicked the brown glass bottles and the sides of the paper packets with her fingernail. She caught the side of a pumice stone with her thumb and her teeth went on edge at the texture of it, its capacity to crumble. You are somewhere between a duckling and a young dog. You have the potential to eat bread and to fetch things.

According to their boxes, all the aspirins in Jenny's house were 'dissolve in the mouth'. Boiled sweets and fudge are sold as 'melt in the mouth' in her school canteen – no doubt there are rules about why these two product descriptions are phrased ever so slightly differently. Jenny imagined such rules were set out by some man working in Trading Standards wearing a brown suit, a green tie and *Ipcress File*-style glasses.

Why would the dip between your upper lip and nose be named after the Greek for *love charm*? Maybe it was related to Cupid and his bow. Again, according to

Jenny's phone and its articles from every corner of the internet: 'each unborn child has an angel teaching them all the wisdom in the world while they are in utero. The angel lightly taps the infant's upper lip before birth to silence the infant from telling all the secrets in the universe to the humans who reside in it.' The grammar of this sentence made Jenny frown and tap her philtrum. She pressed a little harder.

On her tiptoes by the sink, Jenny found her father's old leather washbag behind a row of gummed-up bottles of cough medicine, all four years out of date. The washbag had a broad metal zip, like a pencil case. She took it from the cabinet and felt its pleasing bulkiness. She unzipped it, re-zipped it, unzipped it once more. She enjoyed the *allyup* sound this made, bouncing against the quiet and round ceramic angles of the bathroom. Her mother's washbag was covered in flowers and its zip didn't quite make the same noise.

Jenny lay down on the cool floor of the bathroom and upended her father's washbag. For some reason her father had kept a button and a pound coin in there, which she put carefully to one side, away from the stray pills and puff of cotton wool. She stacked the condoms she found there into a little house-of-cards arrangement. She unscrewed the white bottle of contact-lens fluid and smelled it.

It had been raining all day. It was a cloying, muggy July rain that steamed on its way down because of the heat – Jenny could see drops of it from the floor in the reflection of the cabinet doors, making wet crossbars against the window. It had made the tree leaves stink on the walk from the bus stop.

It had been the sound of the rain against the maths lesson windows that had almost made her miss Vanessa's comment. 'At least I don't have a moustache,' she had hissed at Jenny across her desk. Vanessa's eyebrows had risen and fallen as she said this and then she had looked back at her calculator as if nothing had happened, as if the world hadn't just stalled. Jenny, dazed, found herself blanking out the statement and just staring at Vanessa's eyebrows. They were unsettling, fascinating – little flattish chevrons of hair stark against the smoothness of her forehead. The evolutionary reason for eyebrows, Jenny knew, is to catch the sweat from our brows, providing little weir-gates of fluff to sluice away the worst effects of salt and moisture. But why not then have entirely hairy foreheads? Why do our scalps not reach down all the way to our eyes? Presumably because our brains would overheat if they did not whirr away under that little bared window, that skylight opportunity of flesh above our eyes.

Jenny was touching her upper lip with her mouth fully open.

She picked out her father's straight razor from the floor. It looked as if it would look more at home in a reliquary or a museum than in this room filled with chrome and scented shampoo. Bought as an anniversary gift long before she was born, it was made of wood and metal and had her father's initials worked into it along the handle; to her knowledge he had never actually used it. She unfolded the razor, mimicking the way she had seen actors use them as a prop in Westerns.

When she started secondary school, Jenny could remember feeling her potential opening up in her throat, in her chest, in her head. She felt it physically in her hands as she walked into her first classroom. She forced the fists that she did not even know she had made to uncurl, finger by finger. She now reckoned it must be some kind of excess of this new energy that caused all the other changes to happen to her body that were beginning to preoccupy her and her classmates: changes in body shape, hair, skin, new confusions and obtrusions and outwardlinesses as childhood and its familiarities were left behind.

Vanessa had always managed to detect and comment upon every one of these before Jenny even had a chance to notice them.

In her bathroom, Jenny stood up with the razor. She closed the cabinet doors so she could see her reflection again.

Jenny didn't really believe in God or saints, but she enjoyed praying to Wilgefortis. It was not so much a prayer as a *hello*. She imagined Wilgefortis didn't get many prayers sent her way. Jenny wondered whether anyone ever found Wilgefortis's face miraculously appearing in clouds or rocky outcrops or similar but, because of her beard, mistook the vision for that of Jesus Christ. Jenny had once found a crisp that – in the right light, to a very gullible person – looked a bit like what she imagined Jesus Christ or Wilgefortis to look like. It was a stain baked into the yellow of the crisp. You could sort of make out the eyes, the hair, the beard. She considered selling the crisp to a credulous relic-hunter who might believe the pattern on its surface was significant. On a whim, she had uploaded a photo of the crisp and run it through a face-comparison website. The website had come up with Ralph Fiennes, Robert Redford and Clea DuVall as possible matches to the face found there. Knowing this, Jenny couldn't sell the Jesus Christ-Wilgefortis crisp in good faith.

Jenny listened to the sounds of the water-heater in the airing cupboard next door. The tick of the heater came almost exactly in time with the pulse in her throat.

She observed the pulse. As she watched, either her pulse or the water-heater changed pace. *Philtrum, philtrum.*

Jenny watched the mist made by her breath glaze the medicine-cabinet doors. A question mark of her hair sprung out of its fastening across her forehead.

She didn't blame Vanessa, really. Jenny found she was laid low by all kinds of things nowadays. She had cried twice because of half-caught news features she heard on the radio – a team of thieves had taken to hacking off cows' legs, leaving them to die in the field, because it was easier to run off with just one joint of meat than a whole cow. Ancient, priceless ruins of Mesopotamia had been unwittingly ground up and packed into sandbags by soldiers in parts of Iraq. Hearing both these things, Jenny had not-prayed to Wilgefortis and pressed her philtrum.

Downy. In the maths classroom, as Vanessa looked back to her calculator, the birds had left the tree outside the window in one slow movement, unhurried because of the rain. They had seemed to Jenny as if they were moving in slow motion – sluggish, literally under the weather and shouldering the clouds upward in the wet summer warmth. Jenny thought the whole of July had reeked of static heat. Vanessa's words still hot in her ears, she was aware that she was covered in sweat. With one twist of her shoulders, she imagined that she could wring herself out.

Standing in front of the mirror, Jenny considered whether it would be possible to grow a full moustache before she died. She screwed up her eyes at her reflection and wondered whether she could pull off a handlebar.

Jenny used her father's badger-bristle shaving brush and some yellow soap to build up a thick lather. She said a little prayer, the words of it inexact and unmemorable but straying near thoughts of daughters, and suspension: stretching out one's hands with the palms extended so that an onlooker might not be sure if you were miming holding the world or holding it back. *Wil-guh-fortis, hear my prayer*, and Jenny locked eyes with the bearded face matching her gaze in the mirror, and offered her a shy, sure smile.

Cuvier's Feather

Adding a dash of lilac chalk to the cheekbone will generally make the subject appear ten times kinder. I tend to prefer to use pencil to pastel for courtroom sketches but then there are levels of softness and swiftness to consider. I certainly pick the softer grades of lead and my hands are shiny with graphite by lunchtime. After a full day in court, I am used to finding Batman masks of carbon absentmindedly rubbed across my eyes.

I blow across my chalk pastel picture of you, accidentally harrumphing purple powder over a nearby lawyer's suit.

In your email, you described our first proper face-to-face meeting specifically as a *blind date* so of course within the hour my laptop had grown hot as I busied myself researching your details. Did you know that you share a name with a dentist in Wisconsin? A dentist with big red glasses and a big red dog. That dog is called Astor. According to Image Search, this dog, those glasses, and that dentist pose regularly together in the dental practice's car park.

You were the eighth result.

Some flattering crosshatching will make your hair seem so much thicker, so I really go to town on you.

'And what do you do?' is the way most people phrase the question. I always reply that I am a journalist and add 'but really more of an artist at heart'. After delivering that line, people attempt to strike a balance between polite coos of interest and a *you-pompous-tosser* rolling of eyes, which generally indicates how the night will proceed. If I say directly that I'm a courtroom artist, inevitably the other person just wants to know about any famous cases I have observed and then either make puns about finishing quickly or ask for their portrait to be jotted on a napkin right there at the table. I'm not quite an illustrator, not quite an eyewitness, and art galleries have little time for my portfolio: to claim I'm a journalist with pretensions makes things a little easier for me and harder for others to track me down.

A few years ago, a barrister's wife bought one of my drawings as an anniversary gift. In the picture the barrister was standing, finger raised, during a murder case. Whenever I meet him in a corridor he tells me that the drawing has been framed and hangs above their refrigerator.

On the evening of our meeting, I had run from the Old Bailey so that I would have a chance of getting to the pub before you arrived. Rushing like this, and knowing that I would have to knock dawdling tourists out of my way if I was to make it on time and dodge the traffic as it grows more arrogant as it approaches the City, my final sketch for the day had been hasty, sloppy. I admit I didn't bother drawing the defendant's unpleasant paisley tie or the judge's earrings. Skipping those kinds of particulars always plays on my mind afterwards but at the time it had seemed more important for me to secure a table for our date. I arrived about ten minutes early and chose a place by the bar. My choice was not a good one: not only was my chair right under an amplified speaker, one that made a point of reminding me in blaring tones as I sat down that EVERY NOW AND THEN I FALL APART, but the seats were surrounded by reflective surfaces. My pencil-stained, pastel-thumbed face blinked back at me from the bend of other tables' wineglasses, the polished copper tabletop, the fake horse brasses hanging over the fake fireplace. I couldn't risk going to the toilet and missing your coming through the door so I ground the side of my hand across my nose and hoped for the best. I would have to meet you in Impressionist mode. Later in the evening I remember that I watched you overdo the Tabasco in your tomato juice but did not at the time think it was my place to comment.

Just now on the road adjacent to court, a passing siren started up and caused all of us courtroom artists to jump about a foot in the air. I glance at my neighbour's current sketch: his drawing hand jolted against the page and now the judge sports an accidental bright yellow unicorn horn. Here's something you might not know: in American courts, where I trained, sketchers can draw during the actual court proceedings, but in the good old U of K we must memorise every aspect of the scene, then scamper en masse once the session is adjourned to this mossy paved yard and set it all down. Memorising details and sketching beyond the courtroom walls offers the opportunity to exercise a certain amount of improvisation: for example, a good-looking defendant who winks at me on the way out will have the cut of her suit improved in my drawing, while a juror who elbows rudely past will appear on my paper with an obvious stripe of ankle showing between his sock and trouser leg. Speed is of the essence in sketching so that our final works can be photographed and whisked off to the studio or print room as soon as possible. The nature of this job has prepared me to work well under pressure and to commit visual details to my short-term memory very quickly. It's all about coming up with easily memorable corresponding imagery. We are all fascinating and ugly when assessed detail by detail.

This is how I memorised your parts that evening in the pub:

Dimples – parenthetical
Forehead – the villain's bull terrier in *Oliver!*
Freckles on your forearm – sleet rather than a
blizzard
Eyelashes – ski-jump
Mouth – Holly Hunter; Justin Theroux; my
mother would say it was cruel; clip art ballot-
box tick marks
Angle of chin to neck – egrets; Modigliani
Nose – crumplable; Harold Loeb
Gestures used when describing the recent rain –
Windows98 manicule cursor; Verrocchio's
Christ and St Thomas

Falling somewhere between compiling a blazon and consulting a Rolodex, this appraisal took less than a second. I used to have a friend who was interested in my way of disassembling people's features to remember them; she asked me once to list her details according to this method and sat patiently through my rundown of her face and proportions only to complain at the end that I had made her sound like an exploded lost property department. She then used the word *sparagmos* while ruffling my hair. I have not prioritised looking up that term's meaning but I like the sound of it. We lost touch after I broke her arm that time by the river.

When I implied I was a journalist that evening, you said that you were a professional dog-walker. Earlier that day I had watched you leaving your office on the Strand in a sharp suit with some clients buzzing around you like flies around meat, but at the time I made it clear from my body language that I had not picked up on your lie. I gave that impression, impily implied. You certainly didn't pick up on my lies and the evening progressed genially, easily. You added more Tabasco to your glass while I arranged my smile to its best effect and mentally amended your *Angle of chin to neck* to being 'Modigliani, but better'.

I really am very sorry about the way that I left you in the morning, stealing from your house first thing on a

Tuesday before you woke. The train was full of people on their way to early shifts or sheepishly adjusting their clothing and trying not to throw up. In Waterloo station I always walk directly underneath the huge four-faced clock on the main concourse, used by so many as a rendezvous, and for some reason that day I imagined what would happen if it came loose of its fittings and fell on top of me. In a montage I must have seen in some childhood cartoon, I was certain that if it were to fall to the station floor, the chimes in the clock's belly would sound *When will you pay me?* from the 'Oranges and Lemons' skipping song. Only my hands and feet would be visible under the upturned clock face, sticking out at two o'clock, four o'clock, seven o'clock, and ten o'clock positions. I pulled at my collar.

I suspect the need for my job will disappear in a few years. It's mad, in a way, that we aren't obsolete already: a dying breed, unnoticed crayon jockeys with our vaudeville memory-man skills. In the small outside space by the court where the competing artists scribble away at our canvases, borrowing each other's rubbers and fixatives and mounting our easels for the photographers, the waiting journalists and cameramen treat me as if I was a quaint hangover from another century. They make sure when they shake my hand that my fingers are clean, not wanting pastel residue to clog their Dictaphones or soil their lapels. My profession means that one becomes acutely aware of the rhetoric of dress and posture. After all, that's how I knew from the offset that you were keen on me just from the frequency of hands-to-hair gestures you made in the first five minutes.

Through habit rather than inclination, memories always occur to me as tableaux and frame-by-frame moments rather than as fluid events. That evening in the pub, for example, the devil was in the details and the angel in the angles of your hand on the hot sauce and the botched chiaroscuro of my smudged face; later, a series of images where your mouth became larger and brighter as it drew closer to mine, then, later still, the morning after, the standout picture I take away is of me with my back bent, shutting your front door so slowly and trying not to make a sound. Just now in court I was transfixed by the way the light streamed through the window and became stunted against your cheek as you took the stand.

Of course, it wasn't really you up there in the dock – just someone who looked very much like you. That hardly matters. It's you I'm putting in the picture.

I don't really listen to cases once they are in session because I'm too busy memorising the details of the environment. Sitting through as many hearings and arraignments as I do, one soon realises just how much people shake and the different ways that nervousness or fear betrays itself in a face. I admit that I prefer those scenes to the ones that end with everyone smiling and relaxing in relief or satisfaction: those rarely make for interesting drawings. Everyone always looks like they've slept badly. If I was entirely honest in my drawings, I would run out of blue pastels for the shadows beneath everybody's eyes: I'd run out of blue for the eyelids first, then white for all the hands twisting themselves into blurred, worried polygons in pinstriped laps.

It's not that you have been on my mind particularly, you understand. The person in the dock really just did look a hell of a lot like you.

I told you on our date all about how there are as many fads, regional differences, coteries, and schools in the courtroom-sketching world as any other. I read an article recently which claimed New York courts favour pastels while California prefers watercolours. I am jealous of American courtroom artists because they get to use a lot more orange on account of the jumpsuits; my Faber-Castell Polychromos Tangerine 111 is the most underused pencil in the box. We are all familiar with the limited vocabulary employed by the media to report those people who stand accused in court: 'smirked' is a popular verb, as are the phrases 'hung their head' or 'dropped their head into their hands', both of which I always feel imply that the writer is trying to hint at a guilty verdict, at guillotines or gibbets. So too my pencil- and pastel-led fingers have grown used to describing faces with shortcuts, and every day it feels as if I'm reproducing the same upthrust chin, the same lowered brow. People can be such boringly predictable composites after a while. I used to do caricatures for tourists in Leicester Square. It's a powerful place to be, behind a sketchpad. The friend I mentioned before – the *sparagmos* friend – told me after too much wine that she thought drawing a cruel caricature was like writing a cruel love letter, where the simplest shading of lead against paper could ruin a person's confidence. I liked that. For both art forms, even the blankest looks are busy with ink and the wrong line in the wrong place can change a person's life.

It is hard sometimes not to fall back into a caricaturist's fun grotesques during my current day-to-day. When I got this courtroom gig, I began collecting an album of serial killers' portraits, I suppose to try and see whether I could detect any correlation or make an amateur phrenology of mugshots and find a cheat code for sketching criminals.

The exercise was pointless, of course, and I now use that album to prop up my wobbly desk.

Sometimes I visit museums and sketch the people there, those engrossed in the exhibits as well as the bored, as a way of keeping my talent trained and keeping my eye in: there is a whole canon of beauty and guilt before you hit the gift shop. I practise on the Underground too, where, just as in court, nobody meets anyone else's eyes unless seeking to prove a point. If you spooled a line of wool along each commuter's line of sight, plenty of threads would meet but few of them would tangle. I stare at my carriagemates for a whole revolution of the Circle Line, then spend the next three stops trying to get as many faces as I can down onto paper as accurately as possible. It's good training. Sometimes I guess my subjects' occupations from their dress, along with what kind of house they might live in or whether they are married. Little things. Occasionally I follow a few home to see whether I was right, and for the most part I am. You, in fact, were the first person to notice that I was tailing you from the tube station. I was prepared and so when you turned around I had my story and props ready. I held up my wallet: *I thought I had seen it fall out of your bag at the corner there. No? How embarrassing. I'd better hand it in; do you know where the nearest—? So you live around here? A lovely area. No, a bit further west. Know any good places to catch a drink sometime? Here's my email* and so on and so forth.

It's crucial that nobody ever spots you, lest they start acting up. Keep your head down but take it all in: good advice for life and courtroom artists the world over.

One of the private kicks I get from my job is making embellishments. Look: I'm adding the little badge you wore in the pub to this picture. It's usually cases that have the least media interest that afford me the time to indulge myself, to include things like a doodled spider under a table or the crest on a water-bottle label. A recent tough assignment involved a man who was accused of human trafficking: he had tattoos all over his face, throat and hands. The temptation to just jot down an approximation of a chintzy willow pattern was overwhelming. I hated and loved him for the complexity of it. The shadows that fell under the microphones looked like stretched speech marks as the almost-you answered the prosecutor's questions. The curlicues and flicks of the judge's wig became engrossing landscapes. You can always count on me to catch the details of a courtroom's stained-glass windows, or of an evening, a morning, of pub carpets with their complexities and grimy fuzzes or fuzzy grime. Earlier today, you – the person that looks so much like you – wore red in court. A good move. Red comes across as competitive, puts people in mind of Manchester United, British Lions, Ferrari.

You look best in profile and so that is how I'll draw you up today. I remember that you doubled up with laughter at my bad jokes. By the first drink I knew this would be easy; by the third round I thought it was time to ask you because your hand was near your ear and I knew you would agree; by the twelfth unnecessary vowel of the query, I realised that I needed you to say yes. The adverts on the tube as we made our way back to yours all seemed to be requesting small monetary acts of kindness to be paid to save the bee population, or donkeys, or starving children in war-torn areas because it's only £3 and you're texting anyway.

I'm including your portrait in this courtroom scene and, honestly, for a fifteen-minute job it's one of my very best. You'd love it if you ever saw it: you look just great, confident: the line of your shoulders and your jaw convey that you're assured, *no flies on me*. I've drawn you sitting slightly taller in your chair than is strictly accurate too, but who will pick up on that? In the same way a newspaper editor will not question whether their crossword compiler is making up answers to the clues that have been set, who at the time will nit-pick my pen strokes? It seemed like a big case, so I imagine your head and shoulders will pop up beneath headlines that are meant for somebody else on a breakfast table near you quite soon, or be handed to you in the free newspapers on your way to work. Thank you for all the details: your hand on the glass, your name, your apartment number, the catalogue of errors in the angles as we sat across from one another amongst all those reflective surfaces. It is quite flattering, and unmistakeably you.

Rostrum

Apparently Sue would have to endure the cold morning air of her commute a little longer: the entrance to her office building did not work. *How can an* entrance *not work? Try again, Sue.* The usually automatic, usually sliding doors to the building appeared to be functioning irregularly, refusing to acknowledge her approach. Sue laughed for no one's benefit and advanced, ready to be greeted by the doors' normal hiss and welcoming split, but once again she came up close against the glass screen of them and watched her reflection stiffen.

Sue ran through various second-guessings as she regrouped. It was a working day and she hadn't accidentally misread her calendar. This was definitely the right building, the same one as always, and these were the same doors through which she had sluiced for nigh on seven years. She was awake. She was almost certain she was awake.

Sue planted her feet a little further apart so that her body might become a more assertive shape. During a training day at work some months ago, a bright-eyed external consultant had breezed into the building and made all of Sue's colleagues line up and one by one strike different poses. This was meant to inform or improve office culture, or customer support, or business skills. He promised that after an hour with him they would all not only be able to physically impress a room but ensure that 'clients, onlookers and interlocutors from this moment on will experience value-added comportment denoting frank and open dynamism'. She watched each of her colleagues attempt frank and dynamic standing, sitting down, handshakes, and she listened to the consultant outline how they might improve. When it was Sue's turn, by which time everyone was bored and fidgety, the consultant instructed her to stand as if she were addressing a room full of hostile negotiators. 'Conceive of yourself,' he said, 'as one of life's winners.' She adapted her posture earnestly, keen to please. The consultant tutted then came right up next to her and ducked down, and Sue felt a hand tugging at her ankle, chivvying her leg and foot into a new configuration. She kept her smile fixed for the imagined hostile patrons, and allowed her leg to be redirected. 'Far better,' Sue heard the consultant say, his grip still around her ankle, his bowed head at the level of her hip. There was a warmth in his voice that made Sue dart a glance downward, to see if he was proud of her, but he did not meet her gaze. Sue craned over the top of the consultant's head. The parting in his hair was so neat that long after the exercise was over, after the training day was finished, and over the course of the following weeks, Sue found herself compulsively thinking about it: that neat, clean part in his hair. It intruded on her thoughts as she rode home on the bus, smoothing a seam into a bus ticket with the edge of her thumb. It occupied her as she took a shortcut through the park, following one of the desire paths that communally hemmed and stitched the official landscaping of its squares of grass. She thought of the parting in that bowed consultant's hair every time she passed a framing shop, or saw vapour trails carving across the sky. She couldn't recall what the consultant's face looked like, or what clothes he was wearing, or whether he spoke with any accent or what his name might be, but for whatever reason, she knew that the quality and definition of the parting in his hair would be with her until her dying day.

She daydreamed about the consultant's bedside table. She could envisage such a table quite clearly. It would be neatly arranged with a variety of obscure tools dedicated to precision, which he would apply to his body every morning. Some kind of emery board or sandpaper to buff any creasing traces of sleep from his eyelids; a burin to finesse every pore; he might floss his teeth and between his toes with a fine wire gauge. The parting put her in mind of awls and chisels.

This morning, confronted with the closed doors, Sue thought of the parting in the consultant's hair, his clean hands clasped around her ankle, and marshalled her body into action. She shifted her balance, lifted her chin, and advanced towards the doors once more. They did not respond. Her shoulders drooped as she looked, hurt, at the speckled grey matting of the prohibited floor beyond.

Some unseen, unknowable sensor must be misfiring, Sue thought, or perhaps something as simple as dust or other occluded gubbins jamming the doors' mechanism. Certainly this kind of thing just happened sometimes – it was a glitch, an unfortunate error, and could happen to anyone. Sue tried again and this time she performed a pantomime swing of her arms, as if the problem lay in a lack of momentum rather than perceived conviction, but there was no corresponding twitch of recognition from the office doors, no elegant glide of metal and glass permitting her through. This was dreadful and obscene – a complete joke. Sue looked around. She hoped to meet eyes with a passer-by – a colleague, even! – and establish the whole business as daft and forgivable, or gently unforgettable rather than monstrous, but no one along the busy city street seemed to be facing in her direction. It felt like she was being watched, and the uneasy heat or pressure that surveillance brings to the surface of one's skin lay taut and coiling at her nape, but as far as she could see nobody seemed to be giving her any mind. If anything, all the commuters around her seemed to be pointedly *not* looking at Sue and instead were hurrying past and pulling their coats more closely about their bodies. Sue returned to the doors and gnawed her lip, looking them up and down. Not even a CCTV camera to wave towards, hopefully, apologetically.

Sue pictured her desk upstairs beyond these unbudging doors, beyond the lobby, beyond the lift's familiar wrenching hiss and the carpet-cladded corridors. She imagined the boring, necessary details awaiting her there: her overwatered plant in its glum yellow pot, the faux rose-gold stapler that she bought to cheer up the place. She imagined the Post-it notes on her desk that had lost their gumminess and accrued a fluffy kind of silt along their edges. Another line delivered by the visiting consultant returned to her: *The key to manifesting what you desire is to cultivate the feeling you want to experience.* Sue shut her eyes and tried to *conceive herself* at her desk. The iambs and dactyls of the franking machine sounding down the hallway, the air-conditioned air brittling the surface of her tea … Sue felt her breath steady and, newly galvanised, she stepped again towards the sliding doors. They didn't even flinch.

Sue brushed something invisible from her coat sleeve, extended a hand to the glass of the door as if to rap upon it and then, with a snarl, clamped her arm to her side and tried to take the doors by surprise, shivering forwards once more with an angled shoulder and a grim, set jaw. She made contact with the door and burred its surface with mustered force, but – *and* – that was all.

Sue juddered back on her heel, Sue-in-reflection shaking her head like a stunned, dispirited cartoon of a person.

She approached the doors again, no longer certain of anything, and allowed her forehead and the tip of her nose to press against the cool of the unyielding, unsliding glass. That feeling again of being watched. Sue's reflection squinted at her, then she slid her eyes across the glass to the view of the street over her shoulder.

Opposite Sue's office building, across a rush-hour teeming road, there stood a seafood restaurant. She was used to looking out at this restaurant from her office window. Used to it being there, that is, rather than properly taking an interest in it – just one of the unremarkable facts that upholster a working day. Sue had never considered the restaurant closely and she had never been inside – it was highly overlookable, and after all she preferred to eat lunch at her desk. Recently the office had bought everyone little plastic sheaths bearing the company logo that could be slotted beneath your monitor so that crumbs wouldn't fall into the keyboard. Sue had never thought about it, but now she felt quite strongly that a seafood restaurant in the middle of this non-coastal town was vaguely embarrassing. Looking at her reflection in the awful, clarifying, firmly closed office doors, Sue took in the salmon-coloured swags of the restaurant's curtains hitched up about its windows. She imagined they'd once been white but had been stained by years of steam and kitchen-stink. If she stared in the reflection and really concentrated, Sue believed she could see movement inside the restaurant. The white tablecloths, the dull shine of cutlery arranged on tables. Who went to a seafood restaurant for breakfast? Sue thought, disgusted. Sue glared at her reflection. Sue glared at the reflection of the restaurant across the street. Sue saw there was a woman at a table in the restaurant's window, or the shape and movement of a woman. The woman appeared to be waving, and Sue felt that she needed to be certain, so she pitched away from the unmoved doors and pivoted on her heel.

Although buses and cars and people streamed past, it was clear that the woman in the restaurant across the street *was* waving at Sue – staring, and waving very slowly and deliberately. By the looks of things, even at this distance and at this early hour, the woman was enjoying a huge meal – she had a table to herself in the window, and it was laden with plates and dishes. Although Sue could not pretend to guess exactly what the woman was eating, it had all the fresh pinks and whites and greens and chrome-sheened levels that implied some kind of seafood platter. Sue imagined oysters, langoustines; she felt the sensation of the sting and spritz of squeezed lemon wedges along the crest of her tongue.

Without thinking about it, Sue waved back.

The woman's hand stopped, hesitated, then she was waving again but in a slightly different way. Rather than tracing an arc back and forth, Sue watched as the woman across the street in the restaurant window rippled her fingers one by one through the air. If the hand had been placed flat on a table, it would have made a drumming sound. It was a summoning gesture, camp and delicate, unnerving and beguiling. Without thinking about it, Sue returned the wave in kind, modulating her own hand movement to match the stranger's gesture. She took a step towards the seafood restaurant, glad to have a reason not to further shame herself in front of the closed office doors, and as Sue lifted her foot off the kerb she noticed details about the seafood restaurant that she had never appreciated before: the grey fuzz of smudged chalk on its menu board, the dust clogging its window boxes' artificial plants. By the time Sue reached the traffic lights in the centre of the road, she was close enough to see that the woman waving from its window was about her age, with a similar build and colouring. Her shoulders were perhaps more rounded, and that was surely fair enough as the woman was hunched over her far-too-early lunch. Sue could now clearly see that the woman did indeed have a luxurious and indulgent spread all across her table – or the remnants of a meal, rather, as now she could see that there were piles and piles of discarded bones and scales and shells strewn across the plates and scattered cutlery.

Grunts and squeaks of traffic and the sound of distant horns tuned the air all around her as Sue kept walking across the road, waving and waving. She forgot all about the automatic doors just as they had forgotten about her, and with her head held unnaturally high so that she would be able to meet the eyes of the woman sitting in the approaching restaurant window, Sue kept walking, waving at her advancing reflection. She was close enough now to see that the woman at the table had shelled all the prawns on her plate; in fact, as she drew closer Sue noticed that the woman had slotted each of their bright orange heads onto the fingertips of her waving, waving hand.

The Horticulturalist

It is so difficult to sleep, don't you think, when there is always *something* growing. Thoughts crop up, or spread like something taking root. I might express this better. Thoughts bud, or compost. Thoughts can do all of that. They can become a thicket.

'Deadhead me,' I plan on joking to the Sand-Man when he approaches my bedside. I imagine he might advance with happy tread and readied trug and I would gladly fall into all manner of loamishness. Let's wait for him together.

I was told recently that I should try magnesium as a sleeping aid, but before their sentence was even finished I was already thinking, *oh no*, a deficiency of magnesium can cause yellowed or chlorotic leaves and spotted areas of dead tissue. *Leaf edges might curl.* Other people advise me to count sheep. I try this, doggedly, closing my eyes, and picture serried ranks of thistledown softnesses passing through a gate. I name each imagined sheep after the patron saints of gardening that I can remember – *St Dorothy, St Fiacre, St Phocas, St Valentine, Mr Sand-Man, bring me a dream (baa baa baa baa)* before I realise that my thoughts have moved too far to grazing rumination, which is to say all the good work is undone and I am wide awake once more.

Now here I am, dozily, at work. At *work*-work, rather than working on the garden. My hand is on the counter and my name-badge duly affixed, but in my head I'm wasting time. On the company's dime I'm wasting time trying to remember if there is a fitting French phrase for the joy of wasting time. Because, after all, 'learning French' is one of the things that I've always put off – never had the spare hours, given work, and the garden, and the sleeplessness, and never had the confidence, never the right reason to require it or acquire it or concentrate when there are so many other, more important things to do. I'm sure there *is* a French phrase that is *perfect* for this feeling, but it's just not there at my fingertips or on the tip of my tongue.

The feeling would fall between two phrases that I do vaguely know. They are phrases that occur to me quite often, seemingly unbidden or forbidden or aslant. It feels like an indulgence to allow French phrases to pop into my head so often, a secret patisserie in all the other rubble and the murk, and I check myself and check in on myself, *surely you have something better to do.*

On the one hand, this feeling resonates with the same frustration and indignation as that of *l'esprit de l'escalier*. Whenever I think of the phrase *l'esprit de l'escalier* I have a vision of me in a toga travelling down an escalator – no, not *an* escalator, no; I see the largest single truss escalator in the world, which is in the Bentall Centre in Kingston where I work. In this vision I am travelling down from the food court (and its disappointingly hardened iced doughnuts) to the bank on the lower ground floor. There are many dusty plastic plants there: a weird reversioning of my allotment. In this vision I am heaving forward and rocking a little on my sandalled heels on the escalator's slatted zschushing metal steps, arms crossed, pretzelled, and I am not myself, I am beyond myself or beside myself and I am not wearing my uniform but wearing a toga in this insistent daydream because I am Orpheus, and I am an Orpheus who cannot look back, I cannot look behind my shoulder. That's the image I have when the phrase *l'esprit de l'escalier* comes to mind.

I have worked for so long at the bakery in the Bentall Centre that half of the jobs that I do here are performed through pure muscle memory. I had wanted to work in the shopping centre's bookshop, but the only available job 'for someone with my experience' (what is the French phrase for *zero, zilch, de nada*?) was up here with the doughnuts and the yum yums and the subtle, boring differences between Bath and Chelsea buns.

Last week, my supervisor caught me daydreaming. I was just resting for a second against the till and looking up at the bright, bright glass ceiling of the shopping centre, considering the day.

'If you have time to lean, you've time to clean,' I remember he growled. I snapped to attention and something in me snapped shut forever.

I shouldn't say that he growled. I'd better not. He wasn't beastly, just sinister and lurking and poised, and I'm sure he was right. I think I've been busy looking busy ever since.

As well as *l'esprit de l'escalier*, the second French phrase that is akin (akin!) to this unutterable feeling is *l'appel du vide*. There is a giddiness and an impulsiveness to the feeling. It has a surging, urgent brinkmanship to it. With this phrase and its meaning, I am turned into Orpheus again and I am scratching my Orpheal neck, having pins and needles in my thighs, feeling curiosity fillip a little at the base of my throat as my escalator ticks along.

When I was a child, I overheard some of my classmates discussing bedtimes and the visit of a Sand-Man.

I assumed, not unreasonably, that this Sand-Man was a man made of sand. He would be slightly damp and with a gritty, silicate voice and hourglass waist. He must read the sandpaper, I thought. Nowadays I see this Sand-Man when I am too anxious to sleep and my teeth attempt to grind themselves into dust so that I can make a playmate for him.

When I was slightly older and wondered more about the purposes of things, I decided that the Sand-Man must bring sand to the house as per the milkman, the postman. (This childhood logic did not permit the purpose of *firemen*.) I remember I asked my mother as she plumped my pillow and smoothed my hair: 'Why do we need sand?'

She was surprised by the question but replied, gamely: 'To fill the sand-pit.' This seemed a little circular but I let it slide. 'Did you know,' she continued, 'glass is made when lightning strikes sand?' and out of the corner of my eye, I saw the outline of the Sand-Man blaze and ring out, as if a finger had been pulled across a wineglass's rim. I see this Sand-Man sometimes in the false reflections of a greenhouse on a too-hot day, the edges of his clothes a burnished, fretted fire of fractal scorch marks.

I was never convinced by E. T. A. Hoffmann's fictional Sand-Man. I came across him while at university. I think of this version of an Estimated Time of Arrival Sand-Man every time that I see a crow on the wing carrying something vaguely round, indefinable in its beak, moon-wards.

Sleep as cultivation, landscaping, planting. Last night my sleep had all the qualities of something that is moleish: I really can't say it any clearer than that. Blade-handed, blundering, pernicious – you might call such dreams *restless* but the best metaphor must surely have something to do with moles? It was sable-thick sleep filled with verminous things, undermining, and filled with resented evidences of digging. A corralling or carolling of corollaries of worms. Worms as the opposite of sand.

Where has the Sand-Man got to? As we wait, let's imagine what it is that moles might dream. I would not wish them bright lights, despite everything. I hope a mole dreams deeply. I hope they snore in tiny shunting snuffs.

The Chordettes' song makes the Sand-Man into a kind of gardener. There I am on surer ground. According to the lyrics he can arrange the features of people into wonderful, terrible Arcimboldo blazons – *give him two lips like roses and clover* (*bung, bung, bung, bung*). Perfumed and peppery, polycultural mouths perhaps permit a better kind of dream.

And, just like that, I see him – *don't look directly!* – there – a Sand-Man stealing to my side of the bed. He's wearing chequered silk pyjamas: half man, half snake's head fritillary. His head is bent and nodding on its stalk, knowledgeable as an almanac, my camp little croupier. No – yes – he is a gardener's assistant. No, he would be – *let's stretch and grow deciduous*, eyelids heavy and light all at once, like a bee's progress – he can help pull my gloves about my wrists, tie back my hair – he is making obvious jokes about bedding, where we treat the soil with sharp sand, coarse sand, or quartz sand – a breath hissing like grains through the gloves – perhaps you will see him too, the silks of him, the sapping of the day – *I am sorry for my yawn*, where are my manners? – like dew – where sleep is foraging, a scrumping, a clearing – where sleep is an important draining, where sleep is rootlings, no, a readied plot – a sweet turning-over –

'Positive Feedback': A Game

Number of Players Required: 2+

Recommended Age: -30 weeks +

Players Will Need:

- Time
- Mouths
- Pencil and paper for scoring (optional)

Preparation:

The postures, gestures and facial expressions that are most often associated with the act of yawning are not generally considered to be particularly flattering.

(Reading clumsy and over-elaborate sentence structures can help lug the dull tang of a yawn across one's palate)

(Parentheses as stifled yawns)

(A stifled yawn as breath *sous vide*)

Granted, the lines of a face that might privately once have been considered attractive in some small, world-weary, care-worn way can become emphasised to great effect during the execution of a yawn; overall, however, the revitalisation of one's respiratory tissue through the process of yawning does not regularly present a yawner at their best. If you seem, or a friend/relation/lover/neighbour seems more attractive while yawning, you/they are profoundly beautiful.

This may be a failure on my part, but I cannot quite imagine a horse yawning. During trials in the development of the anti-depressant Clomipramine (trade-marked as Anafranil and Clofranil), test patients of both sexes reported that continued use of the medication in pill form caused inadvertent orgasms when yawning. These last two statements are not related.

My mind is wandering.

Too-quick chicanery of thought can cause a conversational form of the bends.

When I was a lot younger, I attempted to tackle a type of sweet called a 'gob-stopper'. It may well still be called a 'gob-stopper'. I feel about 300 years old wondering whether the word is spelled 'gob-stopper' or 'gobstopper'. I also feel uneasy about the inverted commas. Pedantry can help loop the loose electricity of a yawn across one's tongue. At the time of the 'gobstopper' I was on a school language-exchange programme, stationed at a German town called Boppard. 'Boppard: the Pearl of the Rhine', read the English-language pamphlets on the tourist information desk. I can recommend Boppard's a) riverside views b) riverside benches' paintwork that yielded so easily to new initials in nail-scratched hearts and c) vending machines, at one time filled with gobstoppers and/or gobstoppers. *Zauberkugel, die (Substantiv): harte, runde Süßigkeit. Eine geballert kriegen. Wir bummeln ohne Ziel durch die Stadt.* 'Gob-stoppers' have probably been discontinued on various health and safety grounds; I really do want to emphasise that this was a sweet to be tackled rather than enjoyed. I remember thinking that its English name, *Beano* and Bash Street Kids-y, seemed so at odds with the thing so smooth and glossy in the pick 'n' mix dispenser. Its surface was curdled like Jupiter and it sat as heavy and as flawless as Murano glass in my hand.

That may have been the sweet's attraction at the time: the discrepancy between its name and what I thought was its obvious value. It was not a sweet to share. Everyone had their own. Imagine a whole class of schoolchildren opening their mouths at the same time wide enough for their gob-stoppers; silent choristers, for a second, or as if all caught in the throes of an infectious bout of yawning.

Yawning can look like snarling if one is caught at the right moment. The wrong moment. The first person I kissed lived in Boppard, and they yawned directly afterwards. I doubt they remember this.

Other people's nostalgia can help loose the taut crow's-footwork of a yawn across one's eyelids. Horses yawn when they have liver disease, dogs yawn when they are frightened, fish yawn when they are drowning in air. Do not play this game if you suspect you fall into any of these categories. If you are unsure, it is always best to consult a medical practitioner.

What better time for a game than when you are feeling fatigued? Try yawning now.

Look at the word: yawn. Y-A-W-N.

A lumber of a word. A lummox. Let your mouth and eyelids do the work.

Notes for Players

Note 1: Surroundings
Should the game be played in a place where more than one other person is present, a yawn-rally between the

inter-yawners can be followed by attempts to recruit other opponents. Wittingness and willingness is left to the players' discretion.

Note 2: Scoring an Ace

Skilled players of the game can make more than one person yawn with a single volley. This move gains THREE POINTS so long as it is quite clear who has incited/instigated/procured the subject's/s' yawns.

Note 3: Style

Intermediate players of the game might find that signature moves can be accomplished with greater confidence (and verve!) when supplemented by pandiculation; that is, stretching. I believe that in German, 'pandiculation' is best expressed by the word *Streckung*. Lazy research informs me that this word has a pleasing idiomatic correspondence with *eine Vergrößerungs-oder Verkleinerungsabbildung in der Mathematik* ('an enlargement or reduction figure in mathematics'), a fact that will perhaps help players who are now considering their best plans of attack during a round of 'Positive Feedback'.

I am currently playing a round with an unsuspecting window-cleaner dangling outside my third-floor office. Every time he pulls a vector of suds across the glass panel and squeegees it aside, I yawn. He has not returned the volley thus far. It is a waiting game.

Many baroque and burlesque players of the game aver that noises can assist the contagiousness of their yawn-delivery. I have always found a silent yawn is a powerful gambit. Sighs are on the whole unnecessary, but can prove tactically astute.

Suggested Training

'Positive Feedback' can be played outside, inside, sitting down, standing up, on your commute, on a crucial anxious first trip abroad, alongside pre-prepared combatants or with unaware bystanders.

Should you wish to practise at home, please find below some useful figures from art and history. Players of the game might like to find a decent reproduction of the pieces, cut them out and, limbering, at their leisure, give them a glance for inspiration:

Fig. 1 –
Bruegel's *Yawning Man*, c. 1563
Fig. 2 –
Messerschmidt's *The Yawner*, c. 1770
Fig. 3 –
Munkácsy's *Yawning Apprentice*, 1869

Fig. 4 (economy bumper pack) –
{¬O

The gob-stopper tasted of absolutely nothing. There was a mishap, and now my jaw clicks whenever I yawn. Stay alert, and good luck.

Clarity

Tash's eye opened. After a minute, it experimented with winking.

No need to attempt anything else just yet, Tash reasoned. She had been woken by the bang of the door that signalled she was alone in the flat; for whom, she submitted to the ceiling plaster, would I be getting up? For what?

Perhaps I will never get up from this settee.

That wouldn't be so bad; easier than climbing to my feet at any rate, thought Tash: opening the other eye, moving the arms, all that business with the knees – she imagined that never moving from the settee, never ever, would be far simpler. I suppose I shall get a little thirsty, get very thirsty, then I will simply pass out on this settee and crumble into nutrient-rich, eco-friendly mulch. If you filmed all that and played it back at ten times the speed, Tash thought, the whole process wouldn't take too long at all. The film would start, her eye would open and *poofft!!!* – just a dusty settee.

She would change her answerphone message to explain to all her friends where she was. The council might draw up a petition to move her, to build a bypass through her, but she wouldn't budge.

She swivelled the eye. There was something lying by her head, she noticed, on the settee's armrest.

Maybe if I stayed on this settee forever, Tash continued, my bones might knit and calcify into just one big bone so I *could* never move, only tip and pivot about. My eyelashes might dovetail-joint together and never be prised apart. The earth would crawl up over me, and archaeologists would dig me up in a million years' time, and gasp, and wonder if we were all like that a million years earlier.

Staying on the settee forever suddenly felt like a lot of responsibility.

Her eye realised the thing by her head was a note, pinned right into the leather of the armrest.

Sorry about last night.
I left a sandwich on the side. Hope you like
  pickle!
See you later –

This was followed by the letter *B*.

Had B told her to sleep on the settee? Tash couldn't remember. Maybe she had offered to sleep there, hoping she would get lost down the back of it. 'About £1billion is lost, or lying idle, in the UK's 24.7 million households.' On average, then, how much spare change might be down the back of this specific settee right now? Let me try and work it out, Tash thought. That figure, minus this figure, carry the three.

The eye focused on the wristwatch thwacking out the seconds next to her face. She felt it was safer to check her own watch rather than the clock on the wall; she wasn't entirely sure that time in B's sitting room wouldn't be quicker, or slower, or counting in different numbers.

Quarter past twelve, said her watch. The quality of light through the window meant it must be a quarter past twelve in the afternoon. Good call. Detective skills, interpreting data; a quarter past twelve p.m. She had slept too long.

After a good while of anxious deliberation, Tash decided that her favourite word on the note was 'pickle'. It was fun. The exclamation mark made it even more fun. Pick-le. It was a *pizzicato* word. Pickle: a pink tickle that prickled at a fickle pucker I plucked at, chuckling, truculent. Pickle pickle pickle.

All you need to eat a sandwich is a hand. And a mouth, one presumes. So, basically, B has left a sandwich out for me to show I am not supposed to open any drawers in B's house, not supposed to get my fingerprints on any of B's crockery. B's cutlery. Crockery and cutlery: also lovely words. We have plenty of time before I become as one with the settee, so let's pause and dwell on those words, thought Tash. Crockery, cutlery, cuttlefish in a rockery. Rookery. Cuttleryfish.

A gust of wind sounded outside, and Tash saw lines of rain nuzzling at the window. She imagined the world beyond this room, the street B had stepped out into, a street bulbous and shiny with umbrellas. She thought of all the water that must have hit B in little pieces when B slammed the door and stepped into B's garden, leaving her alone in the flat.

'Hope you like pickle!' the note said. Not, *Do you like pickle?* or *I've put pickle in your sandwich, is that all right?* B was clearly thoughtless to her preferences vis-à-vis pickle. True, the 'Hope you like' was considerate, but the final exclamation mark made the phrase look like it was either trying too hard to please, or else it was a joke. *I hope you like pickle, BECAUSE I'VE ONLY GOT JAM AND BAKING SODA IN MY CUPBOARD!* is what the exclamation mark said. It was manic.

I Hope You Like Pickle!!!!!!!!!!!!!!!!!!!!!!!!!!!!!!!!!!!!!

And what did B actually mean by 'pickle'? Pickle, what a pickle. Some kind of chutney, was it? A piccalilli (piccalilli, Piccadilly, peccadillo, armadillo)? Or a gherkin, a *cornichon*. Americans call gherkins 'pickles', don't they? Don't you have an American aunt, B? B certainly has American trainers; Tash can see them, with her eye, under the armchair opposite her settee. Have your trainers' native Americanisms inked up your bloodstream and into your mouth and your writing fingers? Did you write 'pickle' as an American? Did I fall out with an American last night, me on the settee, you on the armchair? The chair made for your arms. All she could remember was that the discussion had started when B could not find the TV remote, and it had ended – not as planned, with B and Tash together, asleep, ampersand-shaped in a bed – but with Tash waking up alone on this settee reading this note with her one open eye.

She looked at the note again.

Tash noticed B has left her no drink. B wants Tash to desiccate. B wants her kidneys to hiccup and grunt, then wilt inside her.

The eye closed.

You couldn't even be bothered to write your full name. B. Buh. -B-B-B: a string of half-butterflies. 'B': a

Venus of Willendorf in profile. A fat woman with no head and no arms or legs. Your name is sick and a little bit depraved, B.

Her eye widened suddenly. £40 WORTH OF SPARE CHANGE, ON AVERAGE, COULD BE DOWN THE BACK OF THIS SETTEE. I COULD BUY THE WHOLE STREET SOME SANDWICHES OF THE HIGHEST QUALITY ENTIRELY INDEPENDENTLY OF B.

Something quite sinister about the final 'See you later' too. It's the full stop after the letter B. *I will see you later. We shall not meet; I will see you, and that will be the end of it.*

Tash opened her other eye.

Tash got up.

Tash shook all the cutlery out of the drawers in B's flat. She turned the taps on and started the dishwasher, the tray stacked with soap and the door wedged open. She poured some orange juice, which was not left out for her, into a potted plant and put the potted plant in the microwave. Tash made tea with all B's teabags in the sink, with half a bag of sugar to taste; when she found the TV remote down the back of the settee, she put it in the fish-tank. With a pair of Converse shoes. She unplugged the fridge and put the toaster in the bath. This shouldn't hurt B, Tash thought as she did it: B'll notice a toaster in the bath, won't B, before B starts running it? Tash chucked all the crumbs out of the toaster before putting it in the bath, because who could imagine anything worse than a bathful of crumbs?

Tash put on her coat, opened the door, and switched off the light. She paused, then switched the light back on again.

Tash went out into the rain in the front garden, and shut the door behind her.

The sandwich lay untouched on the tabletop, a new note propped beside it. Strictly speaking, it was the same note flipped over but with a new message written on the back.

Dear B, the note read, and no room was left for any words underneath.

Message

Halfway through the lunch it became clear to both of us that watching our food was going to be significantly more important than eating it. I watched the mashed swede harden into firmer huddles around the spinach on my plate; you watched the gauzy twists of steam curling from your sea bream *en papillote* up to the restaurant ceiling. The light changed in the reflections of our knives as time passed, so together we watched that too, and since I had foolishly ordered champagne to the table there were quite a few bubbles to keep our eyes on. Champagne was an oversight on my part. We watched our glasses until even the toughest bubbles had slunk down to the bottom and collapsed into themselves.

This restaurant had been a favourite of ours since we had first become an item, chosen mostly by those who visited for the excellent view it commanded of the bay. I associate it with success and with sweetness. I suppose many couples do. During our early years, a table there was generally way out of our budget but we could kid ourselves that *splurging* became a more dignified, finessed verb if the little complementary bread rolls were just *so*, and when the hand towels in the bathrooms were many times nicer than anything we were ever likely to afford for our student flats. During our first visit we were still in a stage of flirting that relied on finding the same things funny and extraordinary, as we had not yet learned what to be wary of or to overlook as a compromise; as I recall that night there was much pointing out of the misspelling of 'embroiled potatoes' on the menu, and feeling scurrilous for not alerting anyone to the error; a soft upbraiding rejoinder to our own typo'd *I am in my way* instead of *I am on my way* that had been sent in our texts as we arranged times to meet. We made heartfelt, half-cut observations on that first date in the restaurant that 'nothing is as bright as broccoli on a plate'. The expensive hand towels loomed very large, however, in terms of our first experience of the place. Giggling and flushed over a cairn of profiteroles, we loudly whispered a plot to steal them on later visits. We could stash them down our trousers or up our sleeves, we agreed, and amass enough that it would be possible to stitch loads together, incrementally achieving enough material to tailor the most luxuriant of matching dressing gowns. We got to mention the possibility of future dates this way, and the vaguest hint of *your place or mine.* The kind of flirting that is forgivable, maybe, when you're both attempting to share something, anything, and springing at the chance to be giddy and full of gibberish and affection. Completely insufferable for everyone in earshot, but meaningful to those engaged.

That first date was some years ago but we kept a tradition of returning here to celebrate big events: a birthday, a job offer, a successful pitch. The food was great, hand towels unparalleled, and there was that amazing view from the roof terrace. On a clear day like today, if you were one of the diners lucky enough to reserve a table in the right place – or, say, book eight months in advance, just to be sure – it was as if you were sitting in a royal box at the theatre.

Today, this crucial day, we had secured a perfect spot.

'What are we celebrating?' you asked on the way there, checking your hair in the rear-view mirror. I changed the subject and checked that everything I needed for the day was in place.

We were led towards our table by the window. We'd be pressed up right against the view so no one else would have it quite as good. You looked wonderful; I looked acceptable; it was all going great, and would be great, and that was great. Five stars, *ideal.*

'Ideal!' you said as you sat down, letting the waiter pull the chair out for you and then making a wriggled self-conscious bob. I made noises of agreement and smoothed my lapels as if somehow they could have been crushed by anything whatsoever. I glided into my seat, not quite breathing.

'And look,' you said, voice registering surprise as you took in our view. 'Wow.'

I turned to look at what had caught your attention.

'Seems someone's been busy,' you said.

'How did we not spot that when we were parking?' you said.

'I hope they still serve the fish at lunch,' you said.

I stared, willing what I was looking at to not be there.

Of all the days, of all the hours, of all the quadrants of the earth and unravelling excesses of the firmament.

Just as we were about to have lunch, a skywriter had chosen this time and this place to doodle four vast words across our sky.

WILL YOU MARRY ME? the sky asked for all to see.

Someone at a neighbouring table, perhaps reacting to our surprise, leaned across the aisle and said, 'He's been at it for the past quarter of an hour. The pilot, or artist, or whatever.'

From our vantage point, one could just about make out the plane scurrying off beneath the message, a dark dash beneath the question mark's lowest dot. Making a dash for it after shitting all over my expanse of sky with his mile-high puffs of exhaust.

You said, 'Is that right?' and smiled for that person's benefit.

'Sweet,' said the occupant of the too-close neighbouring table.

'How romantic!' agreed their companion, clearly auditioning to be a founding member of a chorus.

I watched you retrieve your phone from your handbag and take a photo of the skywriting which presumably you would never look at again. Then, speaking downwards as if to the table so only I could hear, 'Yeesh,' you whispered. 'Thank Christ *we*' – and here you inclined your head to me – 'haven't got to deal with *that*,' and you inclined your head to the window. The word WILL was visible to me just beyond the curve of your shoulder, livid white against the blue sky.

'No,' I said.

Chintzy music filtered to our table from the lift in the restaurant's lobby, a cover version of a song with no lyrics.

'Yes!' I said again, brightly, shaking my head without thinking that the action didn't match the words.

A waiter shimmered by my side, wearing a suit far smarter than anything I had ever worn in my life and shoes so quiet I did not hear his approach, as if he had slid to us on hidden greased castors or surged to our table on a current of air, borne above the ground. Whichever, clearly he had been busy in some other part of the restaurant, so we got to experience him noticing the skywriting in real time. Really his response to it was rather too much, I thought. He reeled back and, in some kind of ecstasy, he clapped his heart with one hand and used the other to find purchase on the back of my chair. He tipped forward on his toes, like the opposite motion of getting down on one knee, and with this slight elevation took a second to scan the streets below us.

'Can you see the happy couple?' the diners at another table asked.

I shifted my chair infinitesimally, and our waiter jolted on his unsettled wrist, coming back to ground. He said as if to the room in general, and all the cupids hiding in the folds of the curtains, 'If you're going to have graffiti, what could be more wonderful?'

'We'll be having champagne,' I said, defiantly.

'Marvellous,' our waiter beamed, still looking at the sky.

'Definitely,' I said.

It was my intention to propose the champagne like this with authority and purpose, but the way I spoke the words must have made you twig something was amiss; to be so firm about something buoyant, perhaps, struck you as unusual. Your thoughts administered a subtle choreography of your facial muscles. You have always had the uncanny knack of knowing what I am most anxious about at any given moment and for that reason I understood why your eyeline snapped from the waiter to the now-dwindling skywriting message again, then slowly settled back to my face and its margins of error.

'You did *not*,' you said, sounding horrified.

'No!' I said, and I was telling the truth so it felt good, for better, for worse, for richer, for poorer, and so on.

You said with obvious relief, 'No.'

I said, pushing my advantage, 'Out there? Tacky, no? No, no way!'

Your relaxing face seemed to stiffen a little. The hovering waiter distracted me at this point by talking about different bottle recommendations. I said, 'Yes,' curtly and at random to one of the names he read out and he backed away with a grin as large as a hamper, apparently unabashed. No doubt happy to get another chance to look out of the window at the slowly disappearing petition in the sky.

'You wouldn't,' you reiterated, peering out of the window again at the skywritten message. I smiled at you, looking ideal against the view, trying to ignore the scribbles someone else had commissioned scrawled above your head. You frowned at something imagined, perhaps. Then, 'I think I'll have the fish,' you said.

'And anyway,' I said, huffing and puffing and blowing this whole thing out of proportion, 'I wouldn't know where to begin ordering one of those. Planes.'

You scratched your ear.

'Do you get to choose the handwriting?' I continued, not wanting to drop the smile that had worked for me in the past. 'What if the pilot has an untrustworthy way of drawing the letter *w*? Do you get to choose the message, do you think,' you were staring at your hands, 'or is it a set length and wording? They could have put a name at the end, made it more special, but maybe that's more expensive. Or they *wanted* to include the name but got worried a misspelling might ruin the whole thing so dialled it back and just went with the bog standard.'

You said my name aloud, gently, as if calming a dog.

'God, it's bright up here,' I said. I meant to say it enthusiastically. 'Ideal.'

One of the things I love most about you is that you value living with certainty and purpose. Hence my attempt to confidently order champagne: talking like that could fool you into thinking that ordering something, or someone, had anything to do with courage. Your tone was tender when you reached out to take my hand across the table and sought to meet my sun-grimaced gaze.

'You weren't going to, were you?' you asked, speaking lightly, gaily, as if something horrid had been averted and this might all become a fun conversation to remember later, but also in a way that required an answer.

'I wouldn't hire someone to ruin a perfectly nice summer's day.' The table of interrupters had gone quiet in that conspicuous way people do when pretending they aren't listening in. We had done the exact same enough times previously in this very restaurant, so I was familiar with the signs.

You withdrew your hand from the table and extended it to sweep across the fading question, the blotting pad of sky above our reservation.

I examined the chic flower arrangement in the vase on our table.

'Because we said we won't,' you said. 'Wouldn't,' you said.

'Are these orchids, I wonder?' I wondered, in wonder, out loud.

'It's hedge woundwort,' said one of our witnesses, and you said, 'What's that?' and twisted in your chair. Someone from yet another neighbouring table had piped up, a woman with too-big earrings or a too-small head.

'It's hedge woundwort, I think,' this woman said again, excited to be helpful. 'Local!'

'Thanks!' I said. 'OK!'

'We didn't mean to raise our voices,' you said to the woman, apologising for me, and the woman said, 'Just thought you wanted to know.' She may as well have said *tsk* directly in my ear.

The skywriting message was already becoming nothing in the sky, only the *ME?* discernible against the blue.

'It doesn't matter,' I said, but you had to ask me to repeat myself because some wag, some card, some clown from another table thought we were all firm friends now because this one fleeting question was hanging over all our heads and whoever had written it, Trad. Anon., a sociopath, or whoever was patron of its wispy arts intended it so that we all just *had* to bond as critics, and to hell with our private joys and intentions and appetites. A person shouted across to us, waving at our view, 'Do you think someone will have to hire another plane and write back *YES?*'

We all laughed, politely, and I joined in with the laughter to show I was congenial, and relaxed, and I laughed until you stopped. Your laughter trailed off and I stopped mine abruptly. You were staring, I thought, at the side of the table, as if something gross had been left on the tablecloth by a previous diner.

'Anything wrong?' I asked, flapping at the cloth.

'What's in your pocket?' you asked, and my hand sprang to hide the evidence, scrub it from the record.

I don't know much about the wiring of eyes, not even yours, the most wonderful, but there was a flicker there, and an expression of suspicion suddenly became concern, and that concern became resignation.

'We discussed this,' you said.

'A while ago,' I said, as if that was an answer. I did not remove my hand from its place against my pocket.

'I thought I had made myself—'

'You were very clear,' I said, finishing your sentence for you, trying to be helpful. You looked like I had snatched something away, and I saw your hands press against the tablecloth as if to steady yourself, or the world, so I would not attempt to snatch that away too.

'I should leave,' you said, your eyes on the table.

'Are you ready to order?' our waiter said, whac-a-moling up by your elbow and looking thrilled.

'No,' you said.

'Yes,' I said, and we did, and we watched it duly arrive and then watched it grow cold in front of us.

The waiter came and silently tidied everything away. We watched the tablecloth for a while and then watched the same waiter bring us coffee. You took a sip of yours, and then you watched my body language to guess whether I would be the one to try and attract attention for the bill. I kept my hands in my lap. Your coffee cup kept winking steadily at me across the table – on the saucer, lifted from the saucer, replaced on the saucer once again.

'It's good coffee,' you said.

'Can I see it?' you asked and I took the velvet box from my pocket and put it on the table. It was red, clashing horribly with the central flower arrangement. I didn't mean to but I really could not have put the box more perfectly between the two of us, right in the middle of the round dinner table. It could not have been nearer the centre if one of the people at the other tables or the waiter had got out a little protractor, a pair of compasses and made us wait while they did the calculations.

'I think I should be going,' you said, not angrily.

The rim of the ring box was lined with some kind of gold embossing. If you ran a fingernail across it, I'm not sure that the colour would rub away. It looked flaky, by which I suppose I mean antique.

You had your coat half buttoned already, starting the buttons from the bottom of the coat in the way that you always do.

The ignored bubbles in our champagne glasses presumably hissed somewhere down a drain in the kitchen. After a while I released the breath I did not know I had been holding, picked up the napkin that you had squeezed and put it in my trouser pocket. Maybe at other tables hands clasped their cutlery a little tighter, or looser, and soup cooled and glances were exchanged and candle flames didn't waver, unfazed – a whole host of other small, momentous things.

Rituals

This had long been the dynamic between the two six-year-olds: Mark moved and Danny marvelled. At the time, rather than feel ashamed, Danny delighted in the difference between his own relative looming slow-footedness and his schoolfriend's proinking grace. Everyone trips, we all trip, but while with Danny it was all muttered apologies and bumbliclumsiness, Mark made even stumbling look like a virtue; Mark moved like a dream; Mark could never put a foot wrong. It was as if Mark's limbs, cartilage, and bearing had been fed on a diet of words like lissom and lithe and supple. It was as if Danny had learned how to move from the clomping, flailing Popeye or Flintstones cartoons he watched every day, and Mark had learned from documentaries about snakes and air.

Mark was visiting Danny's house for the first time after school, and to mark the occasion Danny asked his mother if they had any Tizer. He knew they did; he had specifically requested it because he knew Mark was coming over and that Tizer was Mark's favourite. He had also made sure that the freezer had enough dolphin-shaped ice cubes, the special ones used for parties, to last the whole bottle, and had taken care and attention to renew the tray in the freezer before he went to bed.

It had never occurred to six-year-old Danny that he should be embarrassed about his home but as Mark raced upstairs and Danny's mother told them she would just be putting the washing up in the garden, he found he was looking around the house with new and disappointed eyes. Newly aware of all the tiny-huge flaws in its décor, smell and smallnesses. The scuffed skirting boards were suddenly unignorable, obviously gross, and the brand name of the soap by the sink was manifestly cheap and inferior. It was clear as day and you could bet a million pounds that Mark's mother had beautiful paintings or interesting posters on the walls of her kitchen, or photographs of Mark being balletic or loved.

In comparison, the 'art' peppered about Danny's home, he now saw, was dumb and weird. His picture of a toucan wearing a hat and holding a cane, tacked up on the fridge: dumb. The postcard from his dad that had a picture of a big red empty canyon, the dustiest thing: dumb. One of the few framed artworks up in the kitchen was particularly embarrassing. Danny must have passed it hundreds of times without really seeing it, eaten so many dinners and frowned over so many homework sums beneath these two figures, but now it seemed to take up far too much wall space. A poster that looked like a print-out of a photo – low-res, grimy stuff – featuring some idiots in suits and shiny shoes caught in the act of pushing each other over. The photo had a caption that began *You Construct Intricate Rituals* ... written alongside the picture on zig-zagging white and black bands of text. The end of the caption was obscured by an ancient, long-forgotten to-do list sellotaped there by his mother: it included the scribbled words 'nit shampoo' and 'malt (?) vinegar'. The idea that puckish, light-as-air Mark could see *this* on the walls of his house filled Danny with a flip of worry. He wished he could reach up and rip the whole poster and to-do list down from the wall, smash the frame, crumple up the picture and hide it in a drawer before Mark came back from hurtling beautifully about upstairs. It was just out of reach, though, tall as Danny was, unless he stood on one of the kitchen chairs.

Danny went to the table and hauled one of the chairs, squealing, across the lino. Trying to be heard over the sound, or trying to mask it, he called out to Mark upstairs with his voice pitched higher and sweeter than he felt, 'Can I get you a drink? We have dolphin—'

There was a slapping, lolloping, awful bang, the kind of sound that makes you pivot towards it. Danny turned, still holding the chair, and saw Mark lying at the foot of the stairs. His friend was face up, his arms spread wide and his school tie flipped up and at an angle across his face. Mark's foot lay resting on the final step, twisted slightly so that his toe pointed directly at the ceiling.

The word for it might be *sprawl*; the word might be *rapture*; the word might be *rest*. Danny looked at Mark and Mark looked like death.

'I'm fine,' Mark said. His eyes were closed.

'Don't move!' Danny said. This was something he felt he had been taught to say, and he said it on instinct while the rest of his body refused to think smartly. His grip tightened on the chair.

'I tripped,' Mark said, which Danny could hardly believe.

Danny's mother was too far out in the garden to hear the commotion, and certainly too far away to hear any shout for help. Danny realised he did not want to shout. He wanted to prove that everything was all right here and that he could be the man who knew what to do in times of crisis. The low buzzing of the fridge next to his arm seemed to fill the room.

'I think I tripped,' Mark said again. Eyes still shut, he propped himself up on an elbow, gingerly, testing the mettle of his arm. 'I'm fine,' he repeated.

In cartoons, the characters always end up putting a slab of meat or a bright red steak against an anvil-bruised eye or a boulder-bumped head. The line sprang unbidden to Danny's lips: 'I'll get something for the swelling,' he said. He wrenched open the fridge. He cast about the reachable contents on its shelves, chucking childish yoghurt cartons and Tupperwared leftovers onto the floor.

Over his shoulder, 'I'm OK,' Mark said again. The idea that Mark was being brave was too painful to be entertained.

Sliding a little on the kitchen floor in his haste, Danny padded to stricken Mark's side and kneeled by his head. He placed an unopened packet of mince on the floor next to them. The label on the clingfilm wrapping said VALUE and BEST BEFORE. His friend opened his eyes, looked at the mince, looked at Danny.

Danny used his fingernails to break the clingfilm on the packet of chilled, taut mince. It was cold to the touch and then not cold at all, and his fingers met the polystyrene container with a muted squeak.

'This will help,' Danny said, leaning over. He was scared but sure of it, and sureness can be reassurance, and the graceful boy let his graceless friend crane his neck and administer to him. Danny scooped the meat into his fist and worked it into Mark's browbone, patting it along the bridge of his friend's nose. The silence did not feel right, and Danny wished there was any accompanying crackle or mindless chirrup of a neighbour's radio, or passing traffic, or even birdsong. 'This will help,' he said again, to fill the space between them, but his mouth was dry and the words came out strangely like a whisper or something intimate. Mark stayed still on the ground, breathing in a shallow trusting way as Danny half coughed, covering his mouth with the crook of his shoulder so he wouldn't have to remove his delicately bloodied fingers from his friend's face. He kept kneading the mince carefully with his fingertips, and with grim-gentle attention was about to begin tamping it over Mark's lips when beyond them there was the sound of Danny's mother coming in from the garden, carrying an empty laundry basket in her hands.

Sonant

This week, I am an editor of laughs.

I am a sound editor. I always hope to be *sound* in the same way that an argument is *sound* – *sound* as in *good foundations* – but what I mean is that I edit sounds at my place of employment. I oversee monitoring the levels of canned laughter before it is added to a TV programme's audio tracks. When I'm introduced to strangers and talk about my job, I often find myself making small *snip snip* motions in the air by way of illustration. I regret doing this almost instantly but try not to let this show on my face until I am home again, playing back the rushes in my head and rescanning the reels of the day. There in the dark I remember the way that my hands imitated scissors or snapping clapperboards mid-conversation. You had smiled as I snipped the air. It was a warm smile, I remember. It was the warmest thing at a cold dinner party. I replay the scene, your warmth and my snipping, and my bedroom ceiling frowns back at me.

Thanks to my line of work, I've heard all kinds of laughs and grown used to their different shapes and flavours, their unique anatomies. The bucking laughs, the buckling laughs, the explosive, and the emphatic and the frantic, the muffled: *HAH, ha ha, ahahahaha, ha-hah, ooo-a, BWHUH*, ha, *ha*, ha, (ha), 'ha', *whuhuh, zchuh* [nasal wheeze], *heh, hoh!, hh, ssSSSSSss-s-s. Aaa.* I suppose I've never heard a bona fide *teehee* in the wild, but like a birdwatcher waiting in their hide, I welcome its appearance someday. I find it hard to imagine a real *teehee* – sharp splutters are rarely attenuated into vowelled wheezes. 'Teehee,' I say very clearly to my bathroom mirror and watch my eyebrows and the corners of my mouth for signs of genuine mirth. It seems more like a sprightly kind of sigh. A wheedling *tsk*.

I only hear the laughs and must imagine what the laugher would have looked like to produce such a noise. I take sly field notes when I'm out of the office. Some people tip their heads back and laugh with hidden loops and stripes of colour in their throat, flattening their tongues and winching their lips in, shoulders juddering: *can can can*. This is a laugh that uses the diaphragm and I think is slightly frightening in its velocity, as if the joke has become lodged in the windpipe and one is struggling to unseat it. Laughter as expectorate, or the laugh as a tickling, swallowed moth, or wishbone.

Someone in the mixing studio at work at work had taken the time to stick a faux-motivational poster to the carpeted wall above the sound deck. It is a simple A4 piece of paper with a Bible quotation printed on it in big black letters, impossible to ignore above my monitor. It reads:

'Ha, Ha'
– *Book of Job*, Chapter 39: Verse 25 (King James Version)

I wonder if the quality of this transliterated laugh changes depending on which edition of the Bible you use. I made a mental note to check if any editors decided against the dry exclamatory 'Ha, ha' and plumped for a 'Teehee'. Some wag had written 'JOB SATISFACTION' next to the quotation in red biro. I laughed the first time that I clocked that, a skiffling type of sniffle or sniffling type of skiffle springing unbidden from my nose. Somebody else had added a smiley face in thick marker beneath the quotation – their marker must have been an old one because the upsilon of the smiley's mouth tapered off into a scattered scratch of ink. You had to be looking very closely at the poster to catch this detail. I only noticed because I was standing on tiptoe and leaning right over the monitor and mixing desk, squinting as umpteen laughs played toothily, toothlessly, tunelessly through my headphones and through my head.

One night while I tried to stare down my bedroom ceiling, wondering for the thousandth time why on earth I had thought it was necessary to mime my job title to someone at a party with that silly *snip snip* gesture, it struck me that the phrase is *canned* laughter rather than *tinned*. I wondered whether the difference was important. What else is *canned*? *Canned* can mean *binned*. Whoop-ass comes in cans, doesn't it, rather than by the binful or baleful or sachet or tin? *Tinny* laughter has other connotations, after all. What do I know about the canning process? Turning in my bed, I imagined the meat and legs of teehee-moths being spat free from audience members' throats and strimmed away, hydrojetted through a microphone's grille so it could be pulped and squeezed through the wires in my headphones.

Another thought intruded: someone at a *snip snip* dinner party once cornered me into a three-hour conversation about organic farming, and I remember them saying too close to my face the sentence: 'If the animals are distressed, the adrenaline in the muscles can be tasted in the meat.' I did not know what to say in response. Possibly I gave a nervous laugh, a small white butterfly released into a gale. The line about toxins and ruined flesh made something beneath my own skin stiffen. I imagined the canned meat of a mothy, mealy-mouthed laugh being scooped up, compacted, seasoned, labelled and made ready for consumption.

All the best laughs that I've ever had caught me unawares, stealing up from my ribs and pinching my eyes into surprised tears. These laughs did not rely on calculation or hyper-attentiveness, nor any pre-prepared *snip snip* gestures. True laughs are unwitting creatures. They are a communication of delight that comes without forethought. You must close your eyes as you make such a laugh as if it is a too-bright thing.

Every day, the leaden stilted false laugh above my work desk: Ha, Ha.

The sheen of tin is so close to silver, but generally cheaper and duller. Easier to produce. Tinny laughs are prized less than silvery laughs, I thought, as the meat of my arms began to relax.

'There's a line from Bergson about the social function of laughter,' said the man at the dinner party, pretending he was interested in my job by telling me he had a more interesting angle on it. He had the look of a man who recited Bergson by heart to people who stabbed the air between dinner guests with scissor-like hands. He also had the look of a man whose adrenaline would never ruin his meat. I envied him as I made my *snip snip* gesture, not knowing how to respond other than by releasing another small white butterfly of a laugh as he drew his face nearer.

It's just a dinner party, I tell myself. *This is not a frightening thing.*

Perform not being frightened at a dinner party for no reason. I continued and concentrated on widening my smile. The lights in the room all felt very bright and winked oddly off the cutlery and off the teeth and in the eyes of the man speaking to me.

There were all kinds of laughter around us in this heaving, genteel, tin-silvery room: some laughs were sludgy with drink but had the bite of desire. Some laughs curdled; others squatted on dinner guests' chests like something from a Fuseli painting, or clambered into ears like heavy-footed gargoyles. Others curved meteoric arcs of delicate frost across the table.

A *claque* is an organised body of professional applauders that are paid to appear in French theatres and opera houses and for a split second, I imagined something similar was happening here: people had been planted purely to simulate real laughs, and they had made a bet that no two would be alike.

'Shall I tell it to you?' the man said.

'Ha, ha –'

Someone across the room chose that moment to give a laugh that was impossible to pin down: it sounded desperate while also plummy and full, and edged with an undeniable horror. Tantalus looking at the suspended fruit from the chill of the river and getting a grip of himself. All around us laughs hid in the folds of napkins and curtains, jockeyed on the pendulum of the mantelpiece clock. It made my head spin. Behind the man's ear I saw the room for a split second in total silence: without sound, with their heads tilted upwards and snapping at the hinges, I saw laughs performed as if each dinner guest was taking greedy, rough bites of the air.

I watched the man opposite me smile as he quoted his philosopher, watched his mouth tightening a fraction with a pursing of pride. I did not catch a word over the laughing roar.

I remember that I nodded and released another laugh-butterfly. Its wings were ragged, and the laugh slipped from between my teeth in a stumbling gawky flight, playing the clown as a defensive mechanism. It was a different species to my first laugh: nervous laughs are not the same as forced ones.

The butterflies snipped the air between us with their wings.

The man looked at me, expecting congratulation.

Beyond his shoulder, I saw you notice that I was trapped. You had overheard the conversation and caught my line of sight – to save me, and make me laugh, I saw you roll your eyes.

Breath left my body unbutterflied, grateful, un-checked.

At work the next day, leaning over my monitor, I took a pencil from behind my ear and squared my shoulders. A new laughter track was in my headphones where it pounded like waves, inking along the folds of my brain. I narrowed my eyes and drew the exclamation marks onto the poster with strong, collected lines.

Ha! Ha!

Words of Affirmation

'No problem!' I said, reliably, dependably to the stranger and she returned my smile with a grateful thumbs up and nipped off to find the café bathroom, leaving her laptop entrusted to my care. She was a young woman, earnest-looking. I guessed she was a student and when I reached over to spin the screen of her laptop a little to get a better view of the document she was working on, I had my suspicions confirmed. I doubt half-written essays on Keats at 11 a.m. are the newest social media fad.

I liked that she made sure to put a deliberately colt-ish, apologetic–appreciative spring in her step as she left my table in search of the loo. This was intended to signal that she valued my time, and to show that she was capable of hurrying when necessary. It was her way of indicating that she would not be requiring my services as bystander or steward for her laptop for too long. *I am quick at urinating*, her choice of pace and gait were intended to convey, *or else I will endeavour to be as quick as possible.*

I had my own laptop out in the café too, so she might have recognised me as a person who knew the value of these things and could handle the duty of care. I examined her laptop on its table next to mine with some curiosity. I wouldn't judge her for the slight scuffing of its trackpad or the sun-bleached stickers on its lid. I suppose I wouldn't leave my iced coffee quite so close to the keyboard, but then I am cowardly about many things – so Terry used to tell me, gently but incessantly – and maybe this person just knows how to live a little more in the moment. I returned to my own work, typing with two fingers.

Of all the people she could have chosen to act as steward, I took some pride at being selected by the young lady. I was the oldest person there. Maybe it was as simple as that, or perhaps I reminded her of a favourite teacher or aunt and seemed trustworthy to her. I looked at my reflection in the chrome buttress of the espresso machine by the café tills: grey hair kept at a practical length, sensible cardigan. That's someone who makes good decisions, I thought, as I pulled her abandoned laptop onto my table to join mine. My husband Terry – married forty years next spring – once used the word *redoubtable* to describe me. He was being sarcastic, and fully aware I was in earshot; it was at the annual church choir barbecue, and I do believe he made his voice a little louder over the sausages spitting on the grill so that I might catch it.

I gave him a meek smile, and he looked back with his usual mixture of sad, bored disdain. We told each other we loved one another by way of habit. We both knew that we used to, and we might as well keep holding ourselves to that: this seemed to be the contract we were living out.

Perhaps it was real *redoutableness* that the young woman sensed about me, and felt would make me unflinching if there was any trouble.

I noticed a spelling error in her essay. I leaned over her laptop and corrected it.

My husband Terry doesn't know I have a laptop of my own. He assumes there's just the old desktop we keep in the study. He also doesn't know that I come here to work. He has this idea that I volunteer at the local gardening club. I'm not too fussed about dissuading him from this belief.

There were quite a few other people working on screens of various types in the café today. At other tables people were sucking their thumbs free of crumbs so that they could unlock their phones. There was the woman by the doorway talking to a tilted tablet who kept sipping her bottle of fizzy water and then wiping her eyes in surprise or delight as if the bubbles were an invigorating shock each time. A young man in the far corner – and it must be said, he struck me as ridiculously good-looking even while eating a powdered doughnut, which is hard to do at the best of times – was wearing so much cologne that I could smell it from here. He must either be getting ready for a first date, going overboard in an effort to impress, or else about to break up with someone and wanting to make it an easier decision for the other party.

With no sign of the laptop owner returning from the bathroom any time soon, I glanced at the barista to make sure they were not aware of anyone in trouble or locked in the loo by mistake, but they seemed very at ease. I thought I heard a toilet flushing or a hand drier blasting, and I arranged my face so I might greet the person who had entrusted me with their possessions with a warm benevolent smile, but no one rounded the corner and returned to the empty chair. Clearly my stewardship should not be considered over.

Terry had always treated the study, and the computer within it, as if it was entirely his domain. He said he was writing a book about military history so justified his hours in there while I went about my day and made sure the house was in order, and our children were comforted when they rang about breakups, or celebrated when they received good news, and that the dog was fed and the cat was fed. All that and more. The usual complaints, the usual mourning, the usual callousing over of expectation and delight. We certainly had 'drifted apart' as they say, and for a long time I couldn't honestly declare that either of us seemed to have the energy to stop that tectonic, redoubtable movement.

Near me, a man with a headset was now talking about offshore derivatives. Looking again around the café, I thought, with no small amount of longing, that we could all take him on if we banded together. We could rip him limb from limb, if we wanted, and made a concerted effort. I returned to my laptop and Googled how best one could go about doing that, and then checked which of the suggested methods would be most efficient.

Still no sign of the laptop owner. I hoped they were all right. Perhaps they hadn't said they were going to the bathroom – did they have to fetch something from another shop? I also couldn't remember much about their appearance; our interaction had been so brief.

To pass the time, I Googled: *how long does average student take to visit the bathroom.*

While listening to a radio programme last year, I heard the words *ventifact* and *dimity* spoken within one breath of each other. My memory for words is not too bad, but the fact I was completely stumped on both rattled me a good deal. I pushed it from my mind, but those two words and the feeling of hollowing doubt kept whirring away through the day. *Ventifact, dimity. Ventifact, dimity.* I found myself saying them on the in-breath and the out-breath. I heard them in the whinge of the weathervane on the shed that Terry promised to oil but never quite got around to doing. *Ventifact. Dimity.* By the end of that day, lying next to a prone and snoring Terry, I was half convinced that the words were meant to be said together and could not imagine one without the other – like *veritable* always comes paired with *smorgasbord* – or as if they were names of lesser known, younger Brontë sisters.

I gathered up my body in Terry's dressing gown (warmer than mine and discarded as ever by the foot of the bed on my side) and went downstairs to the study to find a dictionary, hoping to put the matter and the words' whirlings to rest. Why had I put this off? Why keep these questions safe and unanswered and exquisitely torturous when the solution was right there? When I opened the study door, I remember that I was surprised to see the desktop computer still switched on. Its screen gave the darkness of the study a sterile tinge of colour, somehow like the overhead lights in a doctor's waiting room, which felt at odds with the fustiness of the study otherwise: its foxed books, the threadbare tapestry on the chairs in there and the worn seagrass on the floor. I approached the computer, but I was so unused to even being in this part of the house, unfamiliar with the dips and pivots necessary to get around, that I tripped over some papers. I stumbled a little on the grooves made in the seagrass flooring by Terry's swivel chair, and then I skittered a little on a splayed-open book about Rommel. *Pigsty*, I probably muttered as I shuffled to peer at the screen and see what Terry had last been up to on the desktop.

I remembered it very clearly. It was a website with a pink background and a title in cerise about 'Love Languages' in relationships. I'd heard about this fad before, categorising emotions and desires like this, and I think I probably scoffed a little at the time, but then I had fallen into the habit of scoffing at most things I heard regarding relationship advice just on principle. I was sure if I asked the people in this café whether they found these things useful, they'd answer in the affirmative. *Times change*, as my mother used to say, and her mother before that no doubt. I had adopted more and more of her sayings as I got older, and her Lancashire accent had become more prominent in my own, just as

I recognised more sharply her face in the one looking back at me in the reflections of taps or the liver-spotted lustre of the metal kettle before steam nixed that particular vexation. Other favourite phrases of hers were 'Don't piss on my leg and tell me it's raining' and 'nervous as a long-tailed cat in a room full of rocking chairs'.

She would probably have had some choice words for the person whose laptop I was protecting and who was taking so long in the bathroom, but that's by the by.

I remember that I scrolled through the 'Love Languages' page more to let the surprise sink in than from any real interest. I suppose I felt a mix of curiosity and confusion, and on some level I was trying to square this website and its contents with any possible aspect of military history. There was another tab on the browser, and I clicked that in the hope it might have some answers.

One look was all it took: clearly a site for pornography. I looked away, counted to five, looked back. I felt instantly sorry for Terry. Then furious at feeling sorry. I felt sorry for me. I felt sorry for everyone in the images I was seeing, and then cross for feeling sorry for anyone. There seemed to be lots of animated adverts with looping footage, everything glistening and constant: I felt naïve and intrigued and surprised when all I wanted was *ventifact* and *dimity*. I reached for the mouse on impulse, feeling that I should close everything down at once, but in my haste I must have caught the keyboard with the sleeve of Terry's dressing gown because suddenly I was staring at a list of terms that clearly had been put into this site's search field by a previous user.

I could barely breathe as I adjusted my glasses and peered, not wanting to see.

This was a part of Terry I was not meant to access. This was a part of Terry that was lost to me, that he was trying to find.

I read:

Woman speaking sternly.
Woman stern.
Woman Lancashire accent speaking sternly.

There was a creak of floorboard. I did not need to turn around, but I drew the cords of the dressing gown more tightly around my waist as if it were the cold that made me spin on my heel.

As I passed Terry on the stair, he just stood stock still. I waited for him to speak but of course he didn't. He couldn't. As the couples' therapist our children had researched for us as an anniversary gift but didn't make time to ever quite get around to booking might have said, *Therein might lie the problem.*

I summoned my broadest accent and hissed, with deliberate archness, 'We'll talk about this in the morning.'

I stamped back to bed leaving Terry between the study and our room, neither of us turning our heads to seek out the other's expression.

Where had that girl got to? I checked my watch against the clock hanging on the wall of the café and compared it to the one on my laptop screen and hers. There comes a point where it is an imposition, surely, to assume that people would be happy to spend their whole day watching your things?

We never spoke directly about the search fields, Terry and me. I didn't believe he even clicked on any of the images or videos that his search terms threw up – not anymore, anyway. He just left the words there in the search field, in its little pixelated box, knowing that I'd see them. It was awful, it was stupid, it was sweet.

Woman wearing blue, I read one night, and the next day I found something I hadn't bothered to get out of the back of my cupboard in decades; not fashionable, and certainly nothing out of the ordinary. But it fitted me, at least, and I wore it while cooking the dinner. Terry did not mention it, and nor did I, but he let his hand brush mine while passing me a glass of wine that evening in a way he had not allowed for years.

Woman in Paris (enjoying own holiday), I found in the search field the next night, and without discussing it I booked my Eurostar tickets that evening, opening a new browser tab right alongside his already open one with its pop-ups and pop-outs. I told him my plans to stay for a week near Montmartre over breakfast.

'This is all very surprising,' he said, looking at me over the corner of his broadsheet supplement.

'I can do what I want,' I said sternly, and he ducked his head down, pretending to read the book reviews. In Paris, enjoying the sunshine, I sent him a picture of me by the Basilique du Sacré-Coeur and he responded with a heart. I turned my phone over and went to a gallery – something I hadn't made time for since the children left home.

This way of communicating desires had been going on for some time now. This laptop I had was in fact a direct result of this – I thought I might take him up on the recurrent prompts *Woman surprises herself* and *Spontaneous woman* by getting myself a little shiny 32GB of RAM treat.

I looked around the café. No one was giving me any credence whatsoever: I was thoroughly overlookable. Terry was waiting in the nearby car park. I put both laptops in my bag, adjusted my bright blue cardigan and headed for the door, happy to be reminded that the day should always be understood as a gift.

Fiaschetti

There is a museum in the town of Rutigliano that is dedicated to a certain type of terracotta whistle, distinctive and distinct to the region and traditionally made by local craftsmen. We compared our ability to whistle unencumbered, unterracottled before our visit. You can perform enviably strong whistles by hooking your little fingers into the sides of your mouth and blowing, but I can hum at the same time. There was no clear winner in this contest. The curved plane of a swift shrilled low above our heads. We entered the museum's foyer and got out of the sun.

We had looked forward to this holiday, our first together, in the hope we could unwind: change as good as a rest. You think I cannot sleep because of work stress, or too much screen time before bed. I once mentioned the real reason in passing – the dream I kept returning to, regular as clockwork every night – but as is often the case with recounting nightmares there was no way I could get across to you how awful it was to experience, and how awful to lie with your head on the pillow waiting for it to arrive. It was a dream about an arcade, I said. A posh one in London; they sell very posh macarons. You said that sounded nice, and I changed the subject.

In the museum in Italy, escaping ourselves, some of the whistles on display are as candy-bright as enamel while others are left unvarnished. Some are shaped like birds and warble if the whistler purses their lips just so. One whistle on the shelf is shaped like Silvio Berlusconi clambering out of a lavatory. I do not know what sound this whistle makes when it is blown and I do not ask the attendant. As we stroll down the aisles and aisles and ranks and files of whistles, we are discussing (you are explaining, I am listening) the politics of Toby jugs and Catalan *Caga Tió* figurines. I am surreptitiously trying to whistle and hum at the same time, trying to outdo you.

If you had asked me more about my nightmare, its simple recurrent awfulness, I would have described it as looking exactly like the glass-fronted shops of the Burlington Arcade in London. It's a little walk from Piccadilly Circus and its Eros, surrounded by expensive restaurants and tailors. When the dreams started I hadn't been anywhere near it for years and perhaps by now that part of the city has changed completely, but for whatever reason there's a clear, static version of it that I return to at night. Before I met you, the dream was generally the same: so much to look at and nothing to afford. Something would always go a little wrong in this dream – nothing cataclysmic, no bombs or plagues of rats or bloody rain pouring from the sky – but each time I would wake from them heavy with a sense of shame or self-derision. To recount what happens really makes it sound like nothing: in the dream I will pass one shop selling beautiful leather gloves in vivid colours, for example, where the gloves are all arranged on jointed mannequin hands that look like they are beckoning to passers-by. But as I approach the colour of glove I like the most, I find it has its palm outward as if to halt me. In the dream, the next shop along might have windows filled with silverware but as I peer through the glass all the ornaments and candlesticks seem to blacken or become blurred suddenly with soot. It sounds so stupid, dismissable, but these dreams were awful and were happening nightly, and I couldn't spend a night without returning there.

Our guidebook says that on 17 January every year, Rutigliano celebrates the festival of St Anthony the Great. You may know him, the guidebook says, as Anthony the Abbot, Anthony of the Desert, Anthony the Anchorite, Anthony of Thebes or as the Father of All Monks. According to the guidebook, in art he often seems pestered by all sorts. I wonder if he could whistle well. As part of the day's festivities, we read, Rutigliano hosts a national competition and potters from every part of Italy bring their whistles and exhibit them on the saint's day.

I am not clear what the categories of judgement might be for such a competition: biggest whistle? Heaviest, lightest? Loudest? Most melodious? Which, objectively, is the best terracotta whistle?

The night before our flight to Italy I had woken from an arcade dream, gasping and glazed with sweat as usual. Whenever this happened, I found myself too frightened to close my eyes in case I returned, so I would choose instead to watch the silhouette of your face softened by sleep and count the hours until morning. I thought of our holiday and all the planning you'd done to make sure we could relax. I checked the time on my phone, and crept from our bed as quietly as possible.

Surrounded by whistles, and some paces ahead of me, you're now recounting more facts from the guidebook. One legend persists in Rutigliano, you tell me, that involves a man who survived a terrible fire because of his devotion to St Anthony. In memory of his unblisterment, the miracle of his unscorched flesh and unsinged hair, all the furnaces and ovens should be kept unlit during Anthony's feast day. This limits cooking options somewhat and so traditional dishes comprise dried fruit and puckered-mouth taralli snacks as well as chickpeas cooked with tufa powder, lupins, fennel, celery and a good splash of wine.

I imagine my tooth and tongue against the terracotta stem of a whistle. I might hold it pipe-wise with its colour coating the tip of my tongue. It would taste of things grown in earth, of earth, with earth. I imagine putting each of your fingers into my mouth. You are slightly ahead of me in the museum, still straining to whistle and hum at the same time.

In Rutiglianese, the town of Rutigliano is known as Retegghiéne. Rutiglianese is a Barese dialect which uses this alphabet:

a b c d e f g h i j k l m n o p r s t u v z

I do not know if I can fully conceive of the objectively best terracotta whistle if the letter *w* is not permitted.

I ask you to translate one of the signs in the museum.

You assent and read, haltingly: 'With the whistling whistle of the whistle, lovers could exchange love messages according to a conventional code.'

'"With the whistling whistle of the whistle"?' I repeat.

'You heard,' you say. You have reddened. You do some searching online, and explain the word *siffleur* and the concept of *puirt à beul* to me at length. I have no idea what you are talking about.

As you slept at home, that night before our trip, I stole from our house in a sleepless jag of resolution. I wrapped a coat over my pyjamas and put on my smartest shoes, pawing the destination into the taxi app. They asked for the destination and I said Burlington Arcade – the driver asked if I was sure, as nothing would be open at this time of night, but I said I just wanted to see it. I'm not sure what my thinking was but there was adrenaline in my veins and my mind felt certain – it felt I had to settle a score with my sleeping mind. I would confront the arcade, perhaps was the idea, and stare it down, proving that it couldn't frighten me anymore. We do not live anywhere near the centre of London and this was a taxi ride I could not really afford, especially if we were to have spending money on our trip. I balled my fists in my lap as the cab chuntered and spat through the grey traffic-less early morning.

'We're here,' said the driver, and I stared out of the window, ready for a fight.

The arcade, I found, was boarded up for renovation. The hoarding they used was bespoke and had the history of the arcade printed on it: in my hazy state, I found it hard to take any of it in. Something about a private police force, and that there is a ban on whistling down this single stretch of London street.

The taxi driver brought me back, and I made sure not to wake you as I crept back into bed, warming my feet and hands before I joined you under the covers so I did not startle you. The next day, we are excited for our first holiday together, and I catch you looking at me throughout the day as if to check I am allowing myself to relax, allowing the change of place to loosen something or set something free.

I buy you five terracotta whistles in the Retegghiéne museum gift shop.

That night in the hotel, I dream of taking you to Burlington Arcade. We walk the length of it, up and down, and then you lead me to one of the windows there and turn to face me so I cannot see inside. You let me line a handful of terracotta whistles' stems along your lip, and I watch you take an inward breath.

The Flood and the Keeper

It was growing late and the boy was meant to be revising. He was scheduled to sit three exams the following day – *THREE* – and before any trudge upstairs to bed could be justified, there were biology articles still to read ('Multiple Choice: Adaptations in Mammals of the Savannah'), a passage about *The Impossibility of an All-Knowing, All-Powerful and All-Loving God, Question Mark* that needed annotation and an Eng Lang comprehension exercise that required the boy's close-enough attention.

Competition for workspace on the kitchen tabletop was always fraught and this evening it involved wrestling worksheets from beneath the family's grim-faced orange cat. The boy scanned the Eng Lang worksheet and the stiff little paragraphs sitting on its page. It had no punctuation at all. Presumably the punctuation's absence proved some kind of stupid point; the boy was supposed to add commas and full stops and semicolons and God knows what else in the correct places so that the writing's meaning might be carved or ruminated into easier-to-swallow pellets. The TV in the neighbouring room played something about boats overturning in the blue blue sea, and the boy was so tired of it all, always, all this homework to do. It was just so *arbitrary*. The boy had learned the word *arbitrary* on Friday and was still getting used to practising it in the real world. He really was so tired. The orange cat tucked its head under the boy's hand and, seeing an opportunity, it rolled across the papers and claimed some sort of victory.

The boy pulled the heel of his hand across his eyes in an attempt to juice something like wakefulness from his brain. The text jumped a little on the page as he blinked and the cat snoozed on, face aslant against the prose; the TV continued its report with a soft voice and unfathomable statistics. The boy closed his eyes just for a minute. Propping a chin up on his elbows, just for a quick minute. Just for a whole minute, and it is tedious to recount someone's grammarless and poorly punctuated dreams however baroque or complex they may seem to the dreamer – even though, apparently, most dreams only actually occur in a split second – but! there was a lesson to be learned here! in this one dream! because! this sleeping boy with a sleeping face mere

sleeping inches from a dozy passage about metaphors
and similes dipped into a metaphor or a simile that
began with a conjunction all about enduring narratives
which always prefer carpenters to zookeepers so that
by the time the boy – who was now a zookeeper in his
dream and finding that *he had always been a zookeeper*
with zookeeper's boots and zookeeper's hands –
allowed eyelid to meet eyelid this new-old zookeeper
was trying to parse such terms as 'pitching timber' and
'gopher wood', '2x4s' and 'two-by-twos' passing
around the nearby village by which time it was already
too late for the zookeeper and their favourite animal, a
creature all absurdity and grace that – *would you
believe it?* – only spends between ten minutes and two
hours asleep per day, so that by the end of the first
week of rain in this mere-seconds dream the zookeeper's giraffe was *not* screaming at the water falling from
the sky like the other animals in their enclosures but
instead stood blinking half-dreams patiently in the rain
and blinking at the zookeeper as they pulled on their
waxed hat and their galoshes and began loosing their
birds – all of which they had named, each and every
one – from the cages, and loosing too the lions – which
they had named, each one, arbitrarily – and also loosing
the leopards, and the tiny gryphon, and the bear while
the noise of the village's tin rooves-spelled-with-a-*v* or

roofs-spelled-with-an-*f* grew in full percussion on account of the hail, hail that is not often mentioned in the books that describe the Flood – capital *F* – and its forty days and forty nights, since 'rain' is always the assumption, straightforward, straight-forward, but there was hail too as well as rain and sleet and even silent snow that fell snow on snow in the yard of the zoo as quietly as a giraffe that is sick to its fourth stomach, its second poor simile, its nineteenth hour of rest, and – staring at the endless rain – the giraffe's tall thoughts were interrupted when the zookeeper leaned up to ask, shouting straightforwardly over the sound of water hitting stone and water hitting water, *Who will believe me that you ever existed if none of us are left?* and then the zookeeper was overcome with sentiment and they fetched a tall ladder and the giraffe waited patiently as the zookeeper climbed to its highest rung, reached out, and twiddled the ossicones on the giraffe's head, *ossicones*, the water had ruined every book in the house apart from the dictionary and the zookeeper had been looking up and memorising giraffe-words to pass the time under the weather, *ossicones!*, the little nubs on the top of a giraffe's head, so, here, at the top of their ladder the zookeeper extended a hand and twiddled the ossicones on the top of the giraffe's head and make-believed that by doing so they could radio for help because perhaps the zookeeper was delirious, let's give them that, and they continued seething over the sound of the hail, and then soothing, and then adding, *We share the same number of vertebrae, did you know that, even with your neck so long, I read it in the funny pages* and then the zookeeper made sure that at least the sodden giraffe could have its lunch and together they tongued blossoms through acacia spininess, a treat, and every day in their split-second dream even as the waters kept rising the zookeeper took the time to brush giraffe-dust from the giraffe's coat with the longest broom in the village; last year they had constructed a shed for the express purpose of storing long brooms and the giraffe had watched them build it – happier times – but today, on the thirty-first day if we're count-ing, with the rain that had fallen at first in hyphens or in snow-on-snow asterisks, then falling in en dashes, now in em dashes, and the zookeeper watched all this through long lashes as their shed filled with brooms washed away and they saw what can happen when one overlooks definitions and ampersands and deleaturs and the zookeeper shouted apologies to the giraffe without quite understanding why, and when they were told that the waters would not stop, the zookeeper began killing the animals that would not leave the yard despite being freed, killing them concertedly to spare them from drowning, and of course the zookeeper wept and swore and wept again full sore for the water of all that weeping too and as the new-tides rose the children in the villages did the same to their orange cats and yellow dogs, and a thrush did the same to some snails on a rooftop, and clouds in their bruxism eyed the mountains and set about them in a similar way, and the giraffe ruminated on the fact that even things like the incidental mice in a zoo's yard with its possessive apostrophes must scream and scream and scream at the last, but, the giraffe, in its final moments when the rain grew sharp and italic and perhaps it felt that it could not stay silent without appearing unappreciative as all flesh perished that moved upon the earth, both fowl and cattle and beast and every swarming thing that swarmeth upon the earth, as the dream-zookeeper lost the hand of their dream-wife beneath the water and while the zookeeper was coughing in the dream-water with one arm looped around the parish weathervane, saying goodbye to their giraffe, with a ship, *off there*, just glimpsable in the distance, a ship filled with clipboards and specific animals that do not really have hands so they could not wave back to the zookeeper even in misunderstanding – but for the record it looked a little like that was the case – just as this ship bobbed by, filled with pairs of animals that were somehow believed to be more worth saving, as it bobbed past and beyond the horizon and the men who decided that those animals were the ones who would be allowed to get away while others should be left behind turned their backs so to face their horizon, the zookeeper's shoulders slipped a last crucial inch and it was then that the zookeeper's favourite charge chose its moment and the tall tall tall giraffe turned its funny funny funny head against the zookeeper's cheeks and breathed across their face to keep them warm and the boy woke and forgot the dream just as the background news report ended with so much more work, grammar and paperwork still left to be completed.

What (Not) to Do
With Your Hands When
You Are Nervous

Note One

Let's say I'm currently on the Hammersmith & City
Line and on my way to the British Library. My head is
claggy with admin, studies, nonsense, news. It is just
after the morning rush hour and the carriage is not too
busy. I don't have a seat and I am standing with my arm
raised to keep me steady against the sway of the tube.
In this pose, I need to tilt my head a little to read the
hands on my watch. I have enough room to sway so I
list a little, holding on to the yellow plastic, wipe-clean
overhead strap.

My nails are clean, short.

I am meant to be thinking about Keats or rather
thinking about an essay about Keats. A clean, short
poet, probably. I have written down somewhere on a
bit of scrap paper that he was just over five feet tall. In
1819 while dying of self-diagnosed tuberculosis, Keats

attempted a comic poem, 'The Jealousies'. Who cares?
Not me, and not necessarily Keats: he broke off from
writing – 'Cupid, I/Do thee defy!' – and composed an
untitled eight-line fragment in the blank space on the
manuscript page. Titled posthumously 'This Living
Hand', the poem presents the macabre image of a hand,
both inanimate and animate, alive and dead, seeking out
the reader for an exchange of blood.

Maybe you could recite it to the bump and grunt of
Hammersmith & City rolling stock. I imagine everyone in the carriage reciting snatches of their favourite
poetry along with the rhythm of the carriages, a meter
counted out with dactyls or spondee rattling metal as
we glide-trundle along the gauges of track.

Note Two

I'm running late for a job interview, currently sitting on
a tube beneath London Bridge station. I note that
everyone in the carriage is more attractive than me.
That's fine.

(It is not fine that I noticed.)

Keats trained as a physician at Guy's Hospital not
far from here, and as the carriage idles between stations
I imagine student Keats sitting in some cold, round,
dour dissection lecture theatre. I wonder whether

he ever stole looks at his fellow students from beneath his fringe, or made angry little doodles on his notes.

In his poem 'Hyperion', Keats describes the figure Saturn sitting aghast in the thrall of his thwarted ambition: 'Upon the sodden ground/His old right hand lay nerveless, listless, dead/Unsceptred.' There is a weird amputation of the Titan character here, whereby the hand is viewed as an exhibit isolated from the body to which it is presumably attached.

Whereby. Honestly.

I am so on edge about this interview that I am relying on words like *whereby* to get me through the day and make me seem like I'm worth a damn.

At home, an open tab on my browser leads to an article titled: 'What (Not) to Do With Your Hands When You Are Nervous'.

As a trainee physician, Keats's hand would have been trained ('capable') and ambitious ('earnest') but perhaps overly so ('grasping'). The academic Donald Goellnicht claims that Keats's reason for abandoning a career in surgery might be ascribed to a fear of misdirecting the instrument of the trade in his hands: 'My last operation,' Keats informed a friend in a letter, 'was the opening of a man's temporal artery. I did it with the utmost nicety; but, reflecting on what passed through my mind at the time, my dexterity seemed a miracle, and I never took up the lancet again.'

I will not touch my mouth or hair. These are apparently sure signs I am a liar.

(I will always touch my mouth and hair, I *am* a liar.)

My nails are still short, clean. I'm thinking about my interview prep and 'Hyperion' and Keats and all the hot people on the tube, but I'm also thinking about a joke we used to tell at school: *If you sit on your hands fifteen minutes before filling in an exam, it feels like somebody else is disappointing your teacher.* This was a riff on an older, better-known joke about masturbating.

Note Three

I once found a neat little vase in a charity shop near Parliament Hill. It's made of cool white porcelain and takes the shape of a woman's curled fingers. No idea how old it is.

My mother was always at pains to ensure that I moisturise my hands because 'they are one of the first tell-tale sites of premature aging'. *Thank you, Mother.* The vase is very smooth and I cannot stop sneaking my hand into my bag and touching it.

On the journey here I couldn't help but notice the hands of my fellow passengers: folded in laps, tapping along with an unseen beat, steepled, gnawed. I have grown newly interested in how hands can be used since I met you. It feels thrilling and the best kind of obscene that we get to see hands naked in public so incidentally. Indecently incidentally. *Grasp, clutch, beckon, grip.*

Keats had an express interest in his own physical hand and its physiology. His contemporary Leigh Hunt observed: 'Keats was sensible of the disproportion [...] between his upper and lower extremities; and he would look at his hand, which was faded, and swollen in the veins, and say it was the hand of a man of fifty.'

Note Four

Since writing the above, I have done some Googling about the small vase that I found. It sounds strikingly similar to this product listed on eBay: 'Fresh to the market we offer this rare antique Royal Worcester parian vase designed by James Hadley. This stunning porcelain spill vase is formed as a lady's hand supporting a Grecian urn with her sleeve forming the base and with a jewelled bracelet around her wrist. It is allegedly modelled on his wife's hand and dates from the nineteenth century.'

I imagine a wife's hand replicated over and over and over. Still and chilled and flawless on mantelpieces across the world, holding on to nothing.

In the past I have laughed scornfully at people searching online 'What Do Lesbians Do In Bed?' but I also would definitely click that link.

I touch my mouth and hair. I touch your mouth, and do not care if you are lying.

I do not want to be writing or reading about Keats.

Note Five

Keats's anatomy lecturer Sir Astley Paston Cooper warned his students that 'surgery requires certain qualities, without which no man can arise to celebrity in the Profession – these are a good Eye, *a steady hand*, and above all a Mind which is not easily ruffled by circumstances which may occur during the Operation' [italics my own]. Elsewhere he asked that one brings into synthesis 'an eagle's eye, a lady's hand, and a lion's heart'. It does not seem too far to suggest that Hazlitt's concept of the artist as 'one who is born with an anatomist's eye' might be subtly altered, whereby a poet can be equipped with a surgeon's hand.

In my notes on this, I underlined *lady's hand* not once but thrice. I use words like *whereby* and *thrice* regularly now.

I mentioned previously that the poem 'This Living Hand' was written in the margins of another manuscript. I should have said that it would prove to be Keats's final complete poem. There is a poignancy in the dying poet's appeals for touch within this piece.

After his death from consumption, everything that he had touched in his rooms was burnt.

Before I left you that morning – do you remember? – we played at waltzing in the kitchen, your hand in mine.

Note Six

I am dreaming about your hand. It's a dream, so honestly who cares, but let it show in the minutes that your hand was on my mind.

Note Seven

The author of *The London Dissector: Or, System of Dissection, Practised in the Hospitals and Lecture Rooms of the Metropolis, Comprising a Description of the Muscles, Vessels, Nerves and Viscera, of the Human Body* (Seventh Edition, Revised and Improved, 1826) stresses the specific physical resemblance of the writer's, artist's and surgeon's hands, and the handling of their tools:

> *The position of the hand in dissecting should be the same as in writing or drawing; and the knife held, like a pen or pencil, by the thumb and the first two fingers, should be moved by means of them only; while the hand rests firmly on the two fingers bent inwards as in writing, and on the wrist.*

In terms of my muscles, vessels, nerves and viscera being anywhere near you, I only ever want to revise and improve. This has become a love letter somehow.

(No, it hasn't. It's about my ambition to get better in bed.)

Manuals, handiwork, gesture.

(No, it isn't. This is all just distraction.)

(It has been a while since I touched anyone.)

Note Eight

There's a letter Keats wrote in 1819:

*From the time you left me, our friends say that I
have altered completely, am not the same person
… I daresay you have altered also – every man
does – our bodies every seven years are completely
fresh-material'd – seven years ago it was not this
hand that clench'd itself against Hammond …
'Tis an uneasy thought that in seven years the
same hands cannot greet themselves again. All
this may be obviated by a wilful and dramatic
exercise of our Minds toward one another.*

Wish you were here x

Note Nine

I have had quite enough of paperwork but I had to
write to tell you I came across a legal phrase today:
mortmain. It refers to a posthumous control exercised
by a testator over the uses to which the property is to
be applied. I know, I almost fell asleep reading that too.
But the term literally means *dead hand*. Hands as pulsing, prolonging, dextrous, distant, inching closer.

The disembodied hand has a long history in litera-
ture; the 'beast with five fingers' tale (a label borrowed
from William Fryer Harvey's 1920s pastiche of this
genre) revolves around wandering, severed hands. You
know the kind of thing. Thing from the Addams

Family is a fan favourite. On Wikipedia, I note its full name is given as 'Thing T. Thing'.

In my notes, I've quoted a scholar called Hopkins (*waves*), who alludes to Wittgenstein (*handshakes*) and his use of a hypothetical philosopher (*thumbs nose*) who 'tries to bring out the relation between name and thing by staring at an object in front of him and repeating the name or the word "this" innumerable times'. By doing so, the object and its designated name become even more alien.

I want this, I want it, I want you, I want that, I know how to do this, I want to know how to do that.

Things can be warm and capable, earnest, grasping, all the et ceteras.

Hands have become wonderful and strange since I met you.

See you when I see you.

Yours,

Hare and Hounds

Mr Warringer's desk in the art department afforded him an excellent vantage point for watching the race. It was quite a cold day and the radiators beneath the window-pane were making their own spectator hoodlum noises deep in their throats, causing condensation on the windows. Mr Warringer had to wipe his sleeve across the glass every five minutes to ensure he had a clear line of sight. He didn't know he was doing it. The sound of these radiators, and the action of his sleeve against the window, were a constant in his life. The radiators were iron but painted over with decades' worth of white paint and, although Mr Warringer had forgotten, when he'd been a pupil at the school this very same classroom used to be annexed for History lessons – during a half-hour lecture about French tax legislation, young Warringer had scratched his initials into the yielding surface of the radiators with a pair of compasses. Over the years his letters had been incorporated into some other boy's scratched expletive. In turn this had then grown a speech bubble around it and become part of a game of hangman. Marks handed down and repurposed, boredom relentless.

The sleeve of his uniform against the fogged pane, *weep weep*. The sleeve of his suit jacket against the glass, *weep weep*. Mr Warringer spotted the lone runner out in the field, the boy's white vest and socks stark against the grass.

It was the school's annual 'hare and hounds' contest, held every May Day whatever the weather and with great internal build-up. It was generally intended and presumably maintained because it provided a bit of light relief for the boys before exam season, but as with any tradition it was also imbued with a very specific kind of ritual power. Certainly, it was treated by many of the members of staff as if it were a highlight not only of the term's calendar but of the boys' lives, with winners' names engraved on a succession of special *Hare* cups and plates, with surnames going all the way back to 1855, and there was usually a photo taken for the local newspaper. From his time spent as both pupil and schoolmaster, Mr Warringer also knew that both the teachers and the boys ran various secretive but lucrative betting pools based on projected outcomes of the race, and some years the stakes were not low in terms of money and social capital.

Mr Warringer watched the lone athlete readjust the satchel slung across his shoulders. He remembered the serrated pressure of its strap against the flesh of his own neck so many years ago.

Nothing has changed about the school's 'hare and hounds' race in any real respect for hundreds of years, and certainly not since Mr Warringer himself attended as a boarding pupil. He was able to attend due to a scholarship and had to quickly learn how to adopt certain mannerisms and affectations that most of the other children seemed to already know by heart. The 'hare and hounds' was one of the many institutions that haunted the walls and corridors of the school, bulking out its Wikipedia page and notoriety in the public imagination. It was perhaps more interesting than the fact the boys called the headmaster 'Pater', the sixth form's head boy wore a maroon-banded handkerchief in his top blazer pocket, and the school was once the most expensive in Europe and counted two high court judges, a Chancellor of the Exchequer and a 'gentleman arsonist' amongst its alumni. The 'hare and hounds' race was one of the things that made the school feel like its own fiefdom surrounded by playing fields and boating lakes deep in the Sussex countryside. A dash of the unconventional that was itself unchanging, unwavering; a dependable construct that was catnip for people who thrive on nostalgia and elitism.

The rules of the 'hare and hounds' race are straightforward: one boy from each year is selected to act as that cohort's *hare* and, with a granted ten-minute head start, he must run through the school's extensive grounds to reach the finish line without being impeded by any of the *hounds* – that is, the rest of the boy's year group who follow hot on his heels. Although the *hare* does not need to take any particular route, tradition dictates that he must carry a leather satchel stretched over his shoulder from which he will throw hundreds of pieces of ripped-up paper. This is the trail that the *hounds* can follow, the scent left for the pack to pick up and track you down.

The same rules, rites and routines observed, the same running uniform in the same landscape, as if the race itself is perpetual motion just cycling through a fodder of the newest freshest legs and lungs to keep it going through time.

Officially, today Mr Warringer was meant to be wearing a bright orange hi-vis jacket and acting as a race steward, standing out there somewhere in the sweeping campus at a designated station along the five miles of school grounds to help offer support or first aid if required. This was an innovation brought in ten years earlier after a near-drowning incident when a hound was too keen to snatch the satchel from about the hare's fugitive shoulders. Mr Warringer had been a bystander in this marshalling capacity in previous years and enjoyed the role, clapping the boys as they passed by, giving yawps of encouragement to any stragglers and tutting briskly at any overzealous shouldering or drubbing meted out by the larger, rangier boys who were too pumped by the thrill of the chase and seemed to lose control. He knew the feeling, the giddiness and flash of misrule afforded by the race. However, this year, whether because of the slight sleet or the slight ache in his unfleet shins, Mr Warringer decided that his time might be better spent inside rather than attending to his stewarding duties. He had lessons to prepare for, after all, and reports to write. Paintbrushes to wash. There was time to watch a little bit of the race, however. *Weep weep*, came the sleeve again against the wet glass.

Mr Warringer had been a hare while he was a pupil at the school in one of his first years there, so when he looked out of the window and saw today's single runner making good progress scaling one of the small hills beyond the school's boating lake, apparently heading for the small, wooded coppice, he felt a pang of something like recognised pain or sympathy or memory of strain right across his chest. Mr Warringer gave a short cough to dislodge this feeling.

He recognised the boy, even from this distance and with rain-slicked hair across his face. Sam R from Year 11, wasn't it? Quiet, studious without being particularly brilliant at any lesson; he didn't come up often in staffroom conversations. Mr Warringer had taught him some lessons early in the year about the history of art, and Sam maybe yawned less than most of his peers. Recently, in January, Mr Warringer had invigilated a GCSE mock exam where Sam had been one of the participants – a gruelling ten-hour supervised sketching, based over two days as a trial run for the real thing later in the summer. If Mr Warringer remembered correctly, Sam R had chosen to sketch a still life of some fruit and a hock glass he had bought on eBay and had delivered to the school. All the other boys who had opted for this practical exam, and had prepared a portfolio of accompanying coursework throughout the year as studies and context for this durational final piece, opted to work from photographs or without the need for props. As Mr Warringer recalled, Sam was the only boy who'd wanted to try a still life and was the only one not to listen to music in his headphones over the course of the two-day sketching time. It was quite a taxing mock exam to moderate, as many of the boys had grown bored very easily, knowing that as a mock, the end result wouldn't really matter; Mr Warringer's mouth ran dry from shushing so often from his position by the window, his eyes darting around the easels. Sam had been no trouble, however. Mr Warringer wondered now, watching the distant figure of Sam run its harish way through the green fields, whether the sketching time had allowed the boy to achieve a contemplative moment of silence; something of the long-distance runner's high. Mr Warringer hoped so.

When he had run as a hare, Mr Warringer had been caught in the first ten minutes. The other boys had brought him down with a sliding rugby tackle, hallooing with delight as they screamed their breath and expletives and victory in his face as they piled on top of him, body after body after body. It was the first time he had been touched that year, although he had not known it until that instant. The satchel was wrenched from his neck and exploded its contents into the air, the ripped paper falling all around as the faces appeared in blurred abstracts or extracts: nostrils flaring, all exhalation coming with a judder and vibrato to it. His body was narrated by a fiasco of adrenaline and his breath had tasted of scattershot.

Mr Warringer rose from his desk and went through to the art department storeroom where the boys' work was kept. The cupboards here smelled wonderful, of the cooling moments after industry: pencil shavings, sugar paper, dry clay dust from pots discarded before they were fired in the kiln. He walked along to the Year 11 stack of portfolios. Although there was no rule or contract that said so, it felt unlawful or unethical to go through these things without the express consent of the artists, but Mr Warringer wanted to jog his memory and see what the hare-boy's sketch had ended up looking like after the mock exam. He felt a new affection for the boy, knowing he was one of this generation's quarries. Mr Warringer set about rifling through the reams of paper, staring at labels and looking for the correct portfolio.

Mr Warringer's memories of school were not awful but were certainly not happy, and his part in the hounds' chase had been a clarifying and defining one. It was as if his actual memories had been replaced with some of the pomp and whimsy – it struck him that perhaps that was the reason for pomp and tradition, that it overrode a direct experience of reality by sheer force of a strong brand and the power of a constructed mythos. He remembered crying every night for a month when he first arrived, and the boys in his dormitory politely, terribly, ignoring him. He remembered keeping his mother's weekly letters beneath the trunk at the foot of his bed – imagining he could smell her hairspray on the pages or catch something of her energy and easy grace in the bows and flourishes of her hand-writing. He wished she hadn't chosen pink note pages to write on. Mr Warringer remembered the vertiginous horror when one day he realised that the letters had disappeared, and a greater horror at the thought of asking whether anyone had seen them: the shame, and the longing, and the self-disgust. He remembered sing-ing hymns in assembly and learning that Phelps in 8A could dislocate his shoulders and skip over his own arms. It was all bound up in that cataclysm of being caught as the hare by the hounds: the buttery, scorch-ing breaths heaving from his lungs, the specific embarrassment that his socks had mud on them, the sweat hot and cooling, pooling in his ears.

When he had been caught, rolling in the grass and panting as he was leapt upon, young Warringer realised that the whirling paper, falling all around him as the pack hollered and howled, was pink: the satchel of ripped-up newsprint and old textbooks laced by some unseen hand with his mother's letters.

When he left the school, these were the memories that spurred him out of the door without a second glance. He had sworn never to return. And yet, there he was a decade later interviewing for the role of art

technician, gripping hands with the Pater and all defer-
ence and assiduousness while finding it hard to meet
the older man's eyes, with something like the shame of
the lamed hare making the skin above his collar flush
bright red.

Mr Warringer found Sam's still life stowed in its
portfolio. He held it up to admire it, and saw all its
errors and its potential. He thumbed some grit from
the side of the paper then, gently, slid it back into place.

He returned to the window and drew his sleeve once
again across the glass. He could not see the boy's single
figure anymore – only the trail of paper cresting a hill
and, there, beneath his window, the baying of hounds
beginning their pursuit.

Tether

There was a white balloon and a strange man in my garden, neither one tethered to the other. The moon was as bright and silly as you might expect.

During the evening I thought the air felt charged, as if squaring up for rain or something more pushy. Once the indigos and sky-threads of apricot and pink had tidied themselves away, smoothed and patted down their corners beneath the line of the garden fence, I made sure to stare directly at the moon in case it got any funny ideas. I did not expect a man and a balloon to be there on the patio beneath my window.

I did not look directly at the balloon for fear of bursting it, and did not want to look at the man for fear of fear, so I moved to the centre of my window and glared at the moon instead, treating it as a balloon-by-proxy and ambassador for the man.

'Please leave my garden,' I mouthed behind my glass. It misted over so that the words could not reach the garden. Moon, balloon and man were ridiculous and littering my evening. I rubbed my breath's condensation from the window; momentarily gave the moon new contours with my thumbprint.

Vaguely aware that the balloon was nudging along my garden's back wall, only just skimming the surface of the patio and moving away from the unmoving man, I faced the moon head-on and narrowed my eyes. The moon changed shape against the dark as I squinted – its dot became a dollop and then a mere dash above the clouds. All the white stars and the yellow streetlamp across the road shifted too so that *their* dots became dollops became dashes of light, tessellating and fusing until my eyes were shut and the dark was soft.

The word *dollop* has a pleasing twist of internal symmetry when written down in a recipe. I imagine that if you ladled some moon into a hot pan for a second there would be a flattened amount of liquid in the spoon's bowl and a column of moon suspended between the ladle and freshly poured disc of moon on the pan's surface. Two moon-pools tethered together mid-dollop with the shape of that pour, its architecture possessing a kind of symmetry too.

I can't remember the time I last ate.

I opened one of my eyes. The man was still standing

in my garden. He seemed unaware of the balloon. I hope he did not think I was winking at him.

I am not a good gardener. Some days I wonder if it would be better to say that I attend to the needs of aphids in new and exciting ways. Plants seem to blanch and die quicker in my garden than in my neighbours'. I listen to all the top tips on the gardening programmes, I order the hardiest perennials, browse for the most efficient but ethical pesticides, and make sure to water everything regularly according to taste and need. The soil I buy online is expensive and feels good between my hands, but flowers and plants shrivel here far faster than I would expect. Shrubs' leaves become riddled and splayed, buds bow their heads and fold their chins against their chests in premature defeat. The beans I trained died and left me with only their little wicker teepees draped in brown hollowed stalks. They looked rusty somehow. I grew plants so that through my window, my garden would be words like *lush* and *verdant* and *herbaceous*, but now it's all *skeletal* and *chitinous* and the worst associations with *what's under the patio*.

Was the man also looking at the moon? Was my garden the best spot in the world for moon-watching?

I read an article once in a library, back when I could leave my house and garden. It was by an

Apollo 17 astronaut who claimed the moon smelled like gunpowder.

The white balloon came to a stop in the corner of my garden beneath one of the birdfeeders. I keep these filled with seeds – the feeders' visitors mean that there is at least occasional colour outside my window with the robins and the blue tits and the quiffy, spiffy chaffinches queuing up to eat on the plastic perches. The goldfinches are particularly welcome, as are the wood pigeons who know the difference between *dove* and *dived*. A pair of goldfinches have taken to swinging on one of the feeders in the centre of the patio, getting their heads right against the plastic column of it to gain access to the seeds. That might be their first and only experience of touching plastic, I think. Their swinging action knocks the grain from several of the feeders to the ground, where the wood pigeons are waiting. Even from up here behind my window I can hear the pigeons mumbling contentedly in their throats as they waddle about as seeds fall around their feet as the goldfinches set about their work. I rap on the windowpane whenever a squirrel attempts to muscle in on this relationship but my heart's not really in it. Overall, this year I have found that squirrels, goldfinches, pigeons and moons ignore me. I prefer it this way.

A siren Dopplered some roads away, like sound was rolling away from its own grasp.

I thought the man might be smelling the single white rose by my fence.

As I say, mine is not much of a garden and I am not much of a gardener but one rose did do something like survive this year. It had a small bloom, smaller than a fist, and the colour of cheap vanilla ice cream. Already I suspected I could see an unhealthy tinge and crease at the larger petals' extremities but it was a bonny thing to catch sight of through my window. I fed it cups of bone meal and here it was, smelling of vanilla and bergamot and Christmas and childhood washing powder. I imagined that perhaps this man had passed by my garden, felt the air glitch and fizz with the smell of this single rose in the night, and simply had to investigate. Who knows where he had come from – maybe he had smelled it from miles away, a faint tang or tangle, snagging of scent on the breeze, and he had made it his mission to seek out the source. I imagined him vaulting over hedgerows in the dark, nostrils flared as he dodged traffic and dog-walkers. He might have closed his eyes and decided to trust only his nose as he scrambled over suburban street signs and kerbsides and parking meters. I had not left my house or garden for over a year so I must admit I wasn't too sure of the hazards beyond what

I could see from my window. It's not that I was scared, it just felt safer within the bounds of my fence. I would not want to deny anyone a smell of this single rose. I was proud of it, after all, and it wasn't like he was going to drain it of its scent however hard he breathed it in. I looked at the man looking at my rose and, although he should not have been there, I felt a sudden fellow feeling.

The balloon is another matter. It might snag on the rose's thorns and burst, waking the neighbours or any roosting goldfinches or wood pigeons or aphids. Its deflated white puckered nonsense of a body would then be latched onto the rose's stem and the former balloon, littering even as it littles itself, would be using the rose as a mere prop.

Had the man perhaps *brought* the balloon? It was white to match the rose – was this his idea of an exchange or expression of thanks? It was surely no coincidence that they'd both arrived at the same time in my deadening garden, unless my patio was about to play host to an influx of unrelated objects. The balloon was scudding along the ground in such a way that one could assume it was filled with breath rather than helium. He was a large man, I thought. He looked large enough to fill a balloon with just a few breaths: it would not be so great a gift – thoughtful but not too costly. I wondered if this man's breath might be heavier than mine. He might breathe in great dollops. My breath felt very slight and thin and barely misted a windowpane, even when I was so close to it.

'Is it your balloon?' I mouthed to the window and my breath didn't even register this time, no flare of frost appearing against its surface.

The man looked up. He stared right at me in the window. It was obvious he was not smelling my rose and that he had not brought a balloon to barter for its scent. He was showing he could not only leave his house but also walk down any road he chose, open any gate he wanted, stand in any garden he desired and refuse to smell even its most brilliant flowers.

A new, sudden braveness brought me from the window. It brought me from the window, and so I was at the threshold of my bedroom door, I was at the top of the stairs, I was one hand on the latch then the chain, then the handle of the door and I was in the garden. The patio was cold against my feet and I felt old unpigeoned birdseed beneath my soles.

'This is mine,' I said, not looking at the man. I meant the garden and I meant it firmly but I was reaching for the balloon as the words escaped me.

'Is this yours?' I said, asking the balloon. I took it in both hands so that I was sure it would not slip away. I felt certain somehow that it would make a run for it, bob up and away and nudge its cousin moon in the ribs, laughing squeakily at my inability to leave my bad garden and my house.

It was lighter in my hands than I expected.

'What are you doing,' I said to myself as I tried to twist the balloon, to pierce its skin with my nails. I had a sudden notion that I wanted to flatten it or roll it into a tight, light ball and throw it at the man. Its shape would not budge or squash at all between my thumbs, however. If anything, it felt like it swelled a little.

The man did not move but made a sniffing sound. I hoped he was irritated that I was ignoring him. I could smell the rose from where I was, its vanilla and laundry and clean hopefulness opening the night in half to let something good in. Why was he here, the smell of the rose seemed to say, littering or loitering or opening your garden gate, if not to tell me how perfect your rose was or the light of the moon might be? Did he think he should hop over any fence just because he could? How many gardens and spaces and places had he taken up during this whole year that I had sat by my window counting the goldfinches and the falling seeds, ordering more once the feeders were empty?

I could not seem to gain purchase on the balloon and I wanted to stamp on it, see it flat beneath my feet and darkened in the soil and dust and dirt of my garden. It struck me that I had not eaten all day and I was drunk on the braveness of the smell of the despite-everything rose, and I thought that if I could not burst this hideous balloon between my fingernails that I would bite it, and so I did, I took the smallest nip at the part of the balloon nearest its knot, its neck.

There was no bang and nothing monstrous. I was holding a flat cold sigh in my hands. The balloon did not look slumped or dead, just a wrinkled useless thing in my hands. As I'd broken its surface with my teeth perhaps it was my imagination but I'd felt a fleeting new not-coolness play against my face as someone else's breath escaped and thickened the air. That breath smelled of nothing at all.

I faced the man standing uninvited and strange in my garden, a broken balloon and freed breath between us in the rose-stink and the yellow lamplight. The moon leaned in, perhaps, amongst the unsquinted stars.

It was too dark to make out any of the man's features but I could see well enough to know that he was smiling. I watched him take a step back away from me, towards the garden gate. I held the breathless balloon out to him the very moment that he angled his head slightly to one side, loosened his jaw, took the whole head of the white rose in his mouth, and gently bit right down through its stem.

Moderate to Poor, Occasionally Good

And now the shipping forecast, issued by the Met Office on behalf of the Maritime and Coastguard Agency at 0500 today.

Viking: Southeasterly 4 soon becoming cyclonic 5 to 7, occasionally gale 8, then southwesterly, decreasing 4 later. Rain then showers: moderate, becoming poor.

High Shannon 7 losing its identity [poor Shannon] by 1300 hours tomorrow. High Humber 29 expected German Bight 1032 by same time.

And in a break from our normal forecast, an apology to someone I care very much about and upset earlier this afternoon. Here we go then. I know that you listen to the forecast every day to make sure that I'm all right, so even though we fought I know you'll be listening to this; *especially* because we fought, perhaps. Fought, argued, squabbled, quibbled, severe squalls veering southeasterly: moderate, becoming good.

This morning you slammed the door and I heard you pulling out of the driveway. Perhaps now, hours later, you are still driving – listening to this on the car stereo while the rain bounces off the windscreen in that funny, heavy way it does at night, reflecting the red of street-lamps to hyphens and asterisks.

Thundery showers. Moderate or good, occasionally poor. Moderate to good, occasionally poor.

You realise, more than anyone, that I know nothing about shipping or, really, the sea, apart from the most obvious stereotypes. I've only swum in it once; my family holidays were always by peaks or lakes, not like the white and cyan blue of the coasts I've seen in your family albums. After what happened to us, I doubt I ever will swim in the sea again. But even before, my relationship with the sea was always one of briny stereotypes: I mean, I once ate a whole packet of Fisherman's Friend, that day I met your father for the first time, and I have seen episodes of *Captain Pugwash* and *Popeye*. That's about the extent of it. I remember that the first day I met you, I told you that I thought Popeye looked a lot like Tony Benn. You told me in turn that Popeye's catchphrase, 'I yam what I yam, and that's all that I yam', reminded you of Locke's theory of individualism, and we had both laughed because we were undergraduates in a pub trying to be so clever in front of one another. And yet, for all that cleverness, I have no idea now what *low just west of Rockall 987 expected Bailey* really means beyond the page, beyond this wire mesh of microphone and the walls of this padded studio.

Portland, east or northeast 4 or 5, occasionally 6.

I'm no good if I must veer from a script. 'Not a spontaneous bone in your body' I think is the phrase that you used the day I proposed. You were laughing, and saying yes, but you knew I had spent months planning it all. Three years to the day from our first meeting and you watched me sink to my knee. *Not a spontaneous bone*, you had said, and something tugged in my chest. That tugging feeling is one we've felt all too often in recent weeks. I'm so sorry. More on that later.

I am looking at this script now. Did you know the shipping forecast is set at a strict 370 words? That's 5.8 times the number in the Lord's Prayer and 2.3 times the number of words in the national anthem, even including the verses with the bits about assassins and 'knavish tricks'.

Anyway, now that I've got these fifteen minutes to say whatever I want to you, I'm finding it strangely difficult. Despite that throwaway line about spontaneous bones, you don't react too well to change, I know, so I've probably already stuffed things up by throwing you off course, freestyling on the forecast like this.

Intentions: good. Chance of being forgiven: moderate. Ego: fair, in patches.

The fact I must read this forecast day in, day out to assist other people plan their journeys or feel safe when you are angry at me is an irony not entirely lost on me.

I reckon I shan't be manhandled out of the studio for breaking the patter for quite a while yet. I've gaffer-taped the studio door shut for one thing, which may slow them down a little. A warning to my producers: if they attempt to cut away to 'Sailing By', I'll tell the whole listening nation what the continuity team and the umbrella stand got up to at the annual Christmas party, I swear to God.

So, anyway, I'm dedicating this *Cape Wrath to Rattray Head including Orkney* to my one specific darling listener, to you.

Quite apart from shipping, I find the idea of the sea a funny one. The seas and the oceans are just too big for me to talk about.

Do you remember when on a whim we looked up online how many millilitres of water it takes to drown someone, and the World Health Organisation website came up first, its page featuring the phrase: 'A small child can *drown* in a few *centimetres of water* at the bottom of a bucket, in the bath, or in a rice field.' And we laughed at how specific it was about these three locations, and then looked at one another, appalled?

One can work out how many teardrops there are in the world's oceans: I did the calculation yesterday whilst listening to *The Week in Westminster.* Bear with me, I have my notes here. The volume of the earth's oceans is approximately 1 times 10 to the power 9 cubic kilometres and, if you convert cubic kilometres to cubic metres, and then to cubic centimetres, and then multiply the approximate number of drops of water per cubic centimetre (about 10; at least closer to 10 than 100), you can tell there are approximately 1 times 10 to the power 25 drops of water in the earth's oceans.

In terms of tears, I think together we have managed something similar on a quiet weekend.

There's this idea that in the 1930s, radio announcers were under orders to wear dinner jackets in the evening. I suppose the female equivalent would be ballgowns. I am not wearing either, sorry. I'm wearing trainers. I'm taking off my trainers. How's that for spontaneity? I *appear* to be wearing odd socks.

People listen to the shipping forecast because of its regularity. I think it must work a bit like a lullaby with its meaningless but perfect words said with such certainty. You had a great way of making up lullabies on the spot, bent over the little bed. That's how I think of you, often, the picture of you. But I was talking about the shipping forecast. As well as the triumph of its soothing meter, generally the idea of the sea and what we do *with* it and *about* it is hotching with phrases that delight listeners. A certain comforting familiarity with the phrases of the sea exists generally too: that the 'eights' will come in 'pieces'; there are planks to be walked; thy father lies at full fathom five (*becoming 4 later*); albatrosses will be worn around necks like security passes. Water, water, everywhere, and all the boards did shrink; Water, water, everywhere, nor any drop to drink. You can lead a horse to water, but you cannot make it think.

People are also fascinated by the imagery of the unknowns in the sea and the unknowns in the forecast; the creatures inside it.

Kraken (dormant): rising, expected apocalyptic at 1400 hours: *moderate to severe*.

Who needs fronds with anemones like these?

The forecast, I think, fulfils the role of an incantation, with some faceless, calm entity promising you everything will be all right. It is really just a grown-up's bedtime story, a list of jargon and magic words suggesting that somewhere, someone is concerned with the smooth running of the world.

One of my colleagues once said he felt a certain power came with reading this list of words: he suspected people were listening to him as if he was a Middle England weather god dictating what was to happen, rather than reading out others' best guesses. I think I introduced you to him at the funeral, that colleague. What's that Shakespeare quotation – will I, the newsreader, *drown more sailors than the mermaid shall*?

And lo, it was *good, becoming moderate*.

Personally, I don't think people enjoy listening because of any power play; I think a lot of it is to do with Schadenfreude: people are tucked up toasty in bed with *gale 8 to storm 10, expected imminent* being promised to someone other than themselves outside. The shipping forecast was playing when we arrived home from the ceremony, I remember; playing into the emptiness of our newly too-silent house.

Forecasting has its own appeal as a word. You cast a spell in the same way you cast a net.

I'm not really a forecaster, of course: I just read the words.

Do you remember, my dear, my specific listener, that blue and white mobile we bought for the nursery for above the cot, before we no longer needed a nursery? I said the wooden seagulls hanging from it were flying because I thought they were in the air, and you said the seagulls were bobbing because you thought they were on the surface of the sea.

Maybe you have driven back home and I'm saying this to you from the bedside table.

Anyway.

There are warnings of gales in all areas except Biscay, Trafalgar and FitzRoy.

You give the shipping regions different characteristics according to their names or the memories they evoke for you. I know you do – and I think I can guess them. Viking is obvious, and it computes with the Thor weather-god image I mentioned before; North Utsire and South Utsire make you think of a potential sitcom, no doubt set in the 40s, a bit like *Upstairs Downstairs* crossed with *Dad's Army*. Cromarty is the surname of a librarian who wears cardigans. Or possibly it is his forename – Cromarty Forth. Tyne makes you think of forks and of Newcastle Brown Ale. Dogger is scandalous, Fisher is prosaic. Maybe German Bight makes you think of the neighbours' huge German shepherd that we saw one time in the park as we were arguing by the duck pond; it ran past with a Jack Russell terrier in its jaws. I'm sure you remember. The German shepherd had the Jack Russell by its head, and you just ran over and lamped the German shepherd with your green umbrella while I could only laugh at the horror of it because I was dazed and confused, and medicated, and seeing the scene all wrong, seeing it as if the little Jack Russell was levitating and wearing a novelty German shepherd-shaped hat. I suppose for PR reasons I should call a German shepherd an Alsatian. I would not wish to compromise BBC neutrality.

But anyway, back to the shipping regions. Humber = humbugs for you. Thames makes you think of Wordsworth, or tap water, depending on your mood. Dover is obvious, whilst Wight reminds you of the Dulux colour chart we used for the walls of the nursery, when it was still going to be a nursery. Portland always annoys you as a place name because it sounds like a cop-out. *Port-land*; like *Green Park* and *New York* it seems too simple a name choice for you, as if no real thought went into naming it. Plymouth = obvious; Biscay = biscuits; Trafalgar = the square, and tri-corner hats. FitzRoy I know we both resent, along with the rest of the country, because of the way it supplanted Finisterre, which meant 'end of the earth' and therefore had all the poetry you could want. It is pleasing, and evokes some sense of sated vengeance, that the name 'FitzRoy' means 'bastard son of the King'. Sole = fish, and loneliness. Lonely fish. Lundy is a badly spelled French Monday, whilst Fastnet is a chain of supermarkets, sub-Sainsbury's but one up from Safeway. Irish Sea and Shannon have a pleasing Celtic connection; Rockall and Malin are two glamorous Olympic in-line skaters. Hebrides = your grandmother; Bailey = your grandmother's favourite drink; Fair Isle = the jumper your grandmother gave you the Christmas before she died, possibly on account of Bailey. Faeroes = Egypt, of course, and Southeast Iceland is entirely self-explanatory.

My embarrassment: *low, Rockall, 987, deepening rapidly*, expected home by 0700 tomorrow.

Mood: veering. Defensiveness: backing. *Severe gale force 9.*

Thundery showers. Moderate or good, occasionally poor.

The script says I should close with these lines: *this is the end of the shipping forecast.*

A gale can howl louder than I can. Immoderate, veering westerly, saving something for a rainy day. All the tomorrows still to weather, and voices finding purchase in a storm.

Squared Circle

The signal was not good in this hotel room and even though Danny had paid for Wi-Fi, despite many different tries it just didn't seem to be possible to connect. The annoyance of something unseen and unforceable not working. Danny adjusted his mobile by his chin, as if that would improve reception, and tried the number of the home again.

'We got cut off,' he said. 'Don't worry about video, this will do just fine.'

'That you, Salamander?' came the voice he wanted, that wonderful drawl still identifiable so many years on, and Danny-Salamander was suddenly smiling at the mini-fridge in his room, light-headed with recognition.

Today marked the thirtieth anniversary of Andrew 'Anvil Face' Larsen and Danny 'Salamander' Hobbes's infamous showdown. Even if you're not a fan of wrestling you will probably have seen parodies of it or clips of the fight on one of those *Pop Culture's Highlights in*

Hindsight kind of shows: montages full of dry ice and pumping bass as two men in nylon, Lycra and spandex face each other with guitar riffs and arena-quaking anthems. In footage of the showdown, Anvil Face and Salamander jump on the balls of their feet, primed for the slick slip of synthetic silk draped over oiled shoulders and the puffing thwack of face meeting powdered mat. There's a much-used GIF of Salamander, every inch the young upstart, delivering his knockout blow from that night. The GIF sometimes crops up on Twitter when people want to imply a smooth, total victory. It shows Salamander's teeth bared and his eyes wide open with, depending on the GIF's resolution, his body glitching or gliding forever between his purchase on the ropes, striking his famous silhouette, and his flying, title-clinching leap towards his opponent.

Salamander would not call himself a vain man, but not infrequently he sat in front of his computer watching that looping GIF for ten minutes straight. He asked his son once to show him how to save it and store it on a folder on his laptop. He clicked on the file now as he listened to Anvil Face's voice on the phone, and watched them go at one another over and over and over again.

* * *

At the time of their famous clash in 1993, British-born Salamander had arrived (through a combination of gulping desire, desperation and luck) on the wrestling scene as a huge-shouldered eighteen-year-old with everything to prove; Anvil Face, meanwhile, was a long-standing fixture of the American wrestling universe, a hero of the sport and as old as time itself (fifty-five). The outcome of this match would see the underdog emerge victorious, with Anvil Face forced to shrink back into the shadows to lick his wounds and plan his revenge. Simple stuff. It was a great storyline, simple and rousing, that executives knew would get the ratings. They pulled it off precisely as planned, the crowd went nuts, Danny's life peaked, and his life's trajectory swung to the stars.

Of course the scripted kayfabe for the two wrestlers' showdown had been set in motion months before the night of the fight itself, and the various arcs of their rivalry had been sketched out for them at their very first meeting in the production studio's office. Salamander recalled this introduction vividly: he the young buck with an ambitious agent, Anvil Face the established king of the ring. Salamander had grown up with a poster of Anvil Face on his wall back in Wakefield. It showed the older man executing a perfect mid-diving leg lariat. As far as Danny was concerned, it was a poster of a god – the wrestler's blond hair in that picture a jagged bolt like a meteor trail behind his head.

He was not sure he had ever told Anvil Face about that poster.

Anvil Face had worn a suit and tie to this first meeting. Everyone had. Salamander, wanting to project insouciance and cocksure swagger, rocked up in his training gear on the way to the gym. The shame of this memory still mouldered in Salamander's belly.

'You good?' came Anvil Face's voice down the phone, and Salamander rustled a little in his chair. He shouldn't talk to the memory of the man, he reminded himself.

'Good, sure.'

'Oh yeah.' The sound of a monitor sounded somewhere down the phone; a monitor, or a not-too-bothered alarm. 'You good?'

Salamander had idolised Anvil Face since boyhood, doodling his name on school desks, mimicking every mannerism of his gait and accent, as well as his fighting style and flair for the dramatic. He had imagined what their meeting might be like a thousand different ways, from the pantomime to the romantic, and as they had their kayfabe laid out before them he couldn't believe that this was to be the context for their first introduction. Anvil Face had a great reputation on the circuit as a professional, if a little reserved, hard-working fighter. No further gossip to be gleaned or chewed over. By the time their 'king-slaying' storyline was broached at this meeting, everyone had gone around the room making awkward introductions, which had involved being enveloped and bodily juddered by each other's handshakes.

Danny-Salamander remembered sitting down and trying to feign nonchalance. For some reason he had picked up a huge Coke that morning – he was still new to LA and the size of everything in America staggered him; he felt propelled to be part of the novelty of excess whenever he could. He couldn't believe it when he saw that they sold 64oz drinks at McDonald's, and wondered if he should take the cup back to his motel and repurpose it as a bird bath. *I'll be pissing sugar for weeks*, he said to the woman at the counter, hoping she would laugh, feigning a California accent. Somehow it came out as a weird mix of Texas and Yorkshire but with umlauts. Flustered, he pushed his hands against the Formica countertop so that something distracting happened to the muscles in his arms. The server, already helping the next customer in line, said, 'It's a one-off dino size; tie-in with *Jurassic Park*,' and Salamander slunk away into the hot LA morning. He took one sip of this stupid drink, already exhausted by it, but as some kind of penance he hauled it around all day, in the gym and to the executives' offices. It was flat and warm and gross in every way. He couldn't find anywhere to throw it away before the meeting, and he knew he was so nervous that if he chugged it he would probably be sick, so Danny-Salamander just brought the huge ghastly Coke into the meeting as if this was completely standard for him, completely normal, and placed it on the table next to the catering supply of coffee cups and a tasteful fruit basket. *What was he thinking?* A silly just-shy-of-half-a-gallon of syrup plonked between him and his idol, whose career he was about to unravel.

Their match's storyline was outlined to them, but Danny could hardly listen. It occurred to him with a stab of horror that it might seem like he had chosen to bring this ridiculous silo of Coke to the table as a sign of machismo. Maybe on some level he had. Embarrassing. Amateur. He watched Anvil Face nervously as their storyline finale was explained; he was being told he was for the chop, after all, and for all their agents' and producers' excited talk about narratives and resurrections and projected TV-viewerships, this conversation was effectively a coup for which Salamander was the bright-young-thing face. His idol was being forced into mandatory retirement, and his egg-wet replacement dared to sit across an MDF conference table from him, shaking in his purple Ascis Gel-Lyte Vs and hiding behind a fizzy drink.

Salamander remembered Anvil Face listening quietly to the kayfabe news, then turning his head so that he could look at everyone in the room in the eyes one by one. Then he swivelled and nodded at Salamander's Coke.

'Dino size,' said Anvil Face.

Danny raised his chin, not knowing how to rise to the challenge.

Anvil Face made a movement with his giant, glorious arms and instinctively Danny ducked, but the arm kept going, stretching out as if outlining a slogan on a billboard.

'Catch 'em quick,' Anvil Face quoted, smiling kindly, 'before they're extinct!' and everyone gave each other their laughs and swapped slaps on each other's backs.

'It's good to hear you,' Danny said. 'Sorry, I've already said that.'

'You too, son,' Anvil Face said down the phone. Salamander watched the GIF of them again on his laptop screen. He had to strain a little to hear the voice. 'You keeping well?'

'I am.'

'Get them to put the volume up, can you?'

'What?'

'Never mind.'

'What you say?'

'It doesn't— Thirty years, man, can you believe it?'

'No way.'

For Salamander, it was as if the fight had all happened just last week. To their fans and audience, their characters had circled one another for a good half a year, adopting the swagger of the heel or the clear-eyed naïveté of the put-upon hero, depending on the storyline du jour. Every syllable of mic-snatching braggadocio was written with their final bout in mind; every false tooth spat at the camera, every weigh-in taunt, every flex of muscle, roared invective, and nonchalant toss of wet-look hair was intended to ramp up viewers' expectations of their final battle. Sometimes he could still hear the chant of the crowd in his ears when he did the dishes, and smell the chemical zing of Veet from the dressing room. Prepping before their matches and for photo shoots, Anvil Face and Salamander had always shared tubes of Veet to save money. Anvil Face had hated how long it took to remove all the hair from his body, and often joked that eighteen-year-old Salamander needn't bother.

'Is that why you're called Salamander? Hairless as a newt!' Anvil Face would say and laugh that big basso profundo bellow.

Salamander adjusted the phone again. His hands always surprised him with their signs of age, and he avoided the grey-haired balding man who met him in the mirror nowadays.

'Thirty years. What a thing,' he said. He adjusted the fabric near his neck and felt sweat glaze his fingertips. 'If we'd been married that long, I should be getting you pearls!'

Danny listened out for a smile down the phone.

'Damn right,' said Anvil Face. Something about his voice made Salamander realise that he wasn't necessarily being heard.

'Damn right,' he repeated.

On each anniversary of their fight, Salamander made sure to get in touch with Anvil Face. In the early years the phone calls were brief yelps of victory and mock chiding, a cheeky twang of exuberance and hubris, but as time passed the conversation became less and less about the fight, or even reminiscing about their time in wrestling at all: they caught up about Salamander's children, the weather, a gentle smattering of politics. Salamander's popularity off the back of this fight, plus the combination of his good looks and accent, took him quickly from the wrestling ring to some outer palm-fringed edges of Hollywood where he was cast first as hot baddies, then as brothers of hot leading actresses, then 'Henchman #2' or 'Surprised Glazier', and most recently he had worked as the voice of a haunted lobster in a Lovecraft-inspired indie video game. He enjoyed acting.

By contrast, Anvil Face disappeared from public life almost entirely. He never did return calls from his agent or the Federation about a comeback, and fans never got their avenging storyline for their favourite fighter. Salamander didn't want to pry about the reasons for this, and in their anniversary phone calls it seemed like Anvil Face had started a pottery business, or something to do with kilns at least, at a ranch in New Mexico. He had sounded happy down the phone over the years, and Danny was pleased for him. In interviews, Salamander would always emphasise that they remained close friends, which he believed to be true, even if it was only ever their anniversary phone calls that marked their time together. Salamander had stayed in the US, married and had children, and occasionally he would invite Anvil Face to some of their vacations, hoping that they might gossip about their experience of the industry over hiking trips or boozy cookouts. Anvil Face never did join them, however, and Salamander stopped thinking it was likely. They talked about trips they *could* go on during their anniversary phone calls, however; they even had a running joke about the best way to construct a s'more over a campfire, and Anvil Face gave Salamander's children tips over the phone each year about how best to win games of capture the flag.

On the tenth anniversary of their fight, while Salamander drank a beer and looked out over his decking at his kids, he rang Anvil Face's landline and was surprised that Anvil Face picked up so quickly. 'You been waiting for me to call?' Salamander asked.

'How's my boy?' came the familiar voice, full of warmth.

They talked about this and that, swapped jokes, recipes, sports predictions. Salamander mentioned something about his vague plans for retiring in the distant future.

'Wendy thinks I should commit to a brand and use this handsome mug to sell sell sell,' he remembered saying. 'Protein powders, barbecue grills, action figures: I'll do it all.'

'That sounds great,' Anvil Face said down the phone. 'They'd be lucky to have you.'

Salamander drew on his beer bottle and listened to the crickets outside. 'And how are you doing?'

'There was a guy when I grew up,' Anvil Face said after a moment's thought. 'A big inspiration for me. From your neck of the woods, across the pond.'

'*Wakefield?*' Salamander was surprised, protective.

'No – place called Tottenham, I think?' and Salamander did not want to correct the American pronunciation that put the emphasis on the final syllable. Salamander imagined Anvil Face with a silver rash of stubble, leaning against a window frame somewhere, playing with the cord of the landline. 'Nothing to do with wrestling, but he showed me how I could carry myself, you know?' came the voice down the phone. 'He placed second in the '48 Mr Universe, in the Tall class.'

'Only a bit before your time then.'

Anvil Face laughed. 'When he left bodybuilding, he switched to acting on stage as a strongman. Toured the world with the Folies Bergère troupe in a stripy outfit with a handlebar moustache.'

'Nice,' said Salamander. The air smelled warm, and he was distracted by thoughts of supper.

'He also played Mabel the Gorilla in three *Carry On* films.'

'I'm surprised you know what those are, Andrew,' Salamander said. It was the first time he had ever used Anvil Face's real name. Anvil Face did not seem to notice and Danny-Salamander thought he had got away with it, this hidden secret shared between gods.

'Huge hulking guy with his face hidden in a gorilla suit,' Anvil Face went on, his voice a little dreamy, 'paid to scamper about, completely anonymous.' They both laughed, or allowed the other down the line to hear a laugh. 'Anyway, I think he opened a gym in Tottenham. Wanted to give back to the community, you know.'

'And you want to do that? Start a gym, as you relax in your retirement?' There was a clank of bottles or something down the phone. 'We can drink to that.'

'Not so much the gym,' said Anvil Face.

'Can't see you in Cirque du Soleil,' said Salamander.

'The gorilla suit,' said Anvil Face.

'The gorilla suit.'

The conversation moved on, and the next day Salamander worked out hard in the yard with his skipping ropes and weights, kicking up dust next to the wheel arches of his family car.

In the GIF, Salamander watched the sweat fly from his hair as he sprang from the ropes.

'I'm really sorry I can't be there,' Salamander said to his phone to whoever could hear him.

'He's falling asleep,' said a nurse's voice. 'But he likes listening to you, so keep going if you want.'

'No problem,' Salamander said.

When Anvil Face's neighbours rang Danny up to tell him there'd been an accident, he was confused. He had taken the call in a parking lot in LA; it was a video call, which was a rare thing for him to receive. He wasn't too sure how to work that feature, and as he tried to figure it out he held the handset down some distance from his face. As a stranger's face flashed up on screen, beyond the frame of his phone Salamander squinted at a piece of bright pink bubble-gum fused to the tarmac next to the kerb.

'Hi?'

The neighbours explained the situation, and Salamander watched his own face gasp in the top right-hand corner of his screen. Anvil Face's neighbour also said that his was the only telephone number they could find on the whole property.

'He hasn't been well,' they said. 'Not for a while, you know?'

'I'll take care of it,' Danny said. 'Of course. Thank you for letting me know.'

'Hey, don't I recognise you?' the neighbour said, peering at the phone camera like a dog picking up a scent.

Danny paid for the hospital bills immediately, and tests, and follow-up care. He paid for the monitoring staff. He paid for the nursing home. He asked many times if Anvil Face would allow him to visit, to get some of the old guys from the wrestling days to come visit, but the big man said not to worry, don't worry about that, just let me know how you're doing on our anniversary.

'He says he doesn't want to see if you've changed,' a doctor explained once, while various diagnoses and prognoses were given.

'If *I've* changed?' Danny said, and the doctor looked endlessly tired.

'I wanted to visit,' Danny said to his phone. 'But you know what they say about the best-laid plans. I'm in a hotel just down the road.'

'He's awake again, I'll put the phone closer,' said the female voice. Danny waited.

'Yes?' said Anvil Face.

'I said: I wanted to visit, but I tested positive for the thing going around, so I don't think I should come in.'

'I didn't know you could still get tests,' said the nurse's voice.

'You can,' Danny said. In the GIF, his arm was glistening and crashing through the air.

'Don't you worry,' came Anvil Face's voice, quietly. 'All good here. Thank you.'

'We went out into the garden just this morning,' the nurse's voice added, encouragingly, 'and Andrew was able to name all the birds just by their song.'

'That's wonderful,' Salamander said. 'You're in great hands,' he added.

'You bet,' said Anvil Face and then, with some emphasis, 'The jays here are mighty different to the type you Brits might see.'

'We have the same jays now, man; long time since I've been back home.'

The nurse's voice again. 'I'd never really looked at a jay before, and now I know all about them, thanks to Andrew.' Salamander imagined her by Anvil Face's pillow, or his armchair, holding the phone up, maybe having to talk through a paper mask. She sounded kind.

'I'm really sorry I can't visit,' Danny-Salamander said again.

'No problem,' said Anvil Face.

'I was going to celebrate the big three-oh of our fight,' Salamander said. 'I had a costume and everything.'

'Sounds good,' Anvil Face said. It was the voice of a man who could be any size.

Thirty years ago, Salamander wanted to say to the nurse. Thirty years since our spit flew in each other's mouths and we put false pressure on each other's necks for the cameras. We'll be in our prime forever: me suspended and twitching through that animated GIF, Andrew launching into the wall of some kid's bedroom.

'He's falling asleep again, mister,' the nurse said. 'I know he likes to hear you speaking though if you want. It doesn't matter what.'

Danny thought about what he could say. He could run through the things in his bare hotel room: the coffee machine, the fridge, the stain on the ceiling. He could describe how he wishes he could hold Anvil Face's hand again, his vast terrible hands. He could say how he was wearing a cheap comedy gorilla costume on this phone call but couldn't get the video function to work so thought it best not to bother, stick with the voice. The gorilla costume was insanely hot and Danny had thrown his back out a little wedging himself into it and zipping it up at the collar. He could order the biggest Coke he could find on room service, and list down the phone all the different ways he might have of describing how wrong everything felt.

'Do you know I had a poster of you in my childhood bedroom?' Danny said.

Anvil Face's voice came suddenly clear in Danny's ear. 'Did you hear that?'

'I surely did,' said the nurse, confirming.

'Do you think it was a good picture?' Danny heard Anvil Face ask the nurse.

'You looked great,' Danny said.

'I bet you looked the best,' the nurse said. There was some soft mechanical noise down the phone line, and perhaps the clatter of wheels in a corridor nearby.

'Hello?' said Danny.

'Isn't that something?' Anvil Face's voice again, sounding gentle with reflection. The beeps again, and the murmur of background noise.

'A poster in your room,' Anvil Face repeated. Then the fallen god released a chest-thumping hoot, making Salamander, off guard, sit bolt upright in his chair.

Escape Room

They were only permitted one hour, and their time had just run out. This group had failed in their attempt. I pressed a button on a remote control clenched in the palm of my hand, and the ticking sound booming through the overhead speakers all the way during their session ended abruptly. One of the players gasped into their new silence, as if the ticking had been a shared heartbeat keeping them all going. This gasp folded, could not bear the scrutiny or exposure, and became an embarrassed giggle.

The time limit, of course, was also there to add to the tension. As the players entered the room from the foyer and their time began, the artificial ticking usually got a dreadful-delighted whoop from the participants, chivvying each other into action. An escape room was not meant to be a kind of physical cryptic crossword you could languorously ponder over a long weekend, completing it at your leisure: you were meant to feel rushed, like something was at stake. The time limit was also stated clearly on the booking page when a customer purchased a ticket for their party, and it was on all the promotional material and the posters in the lobby. The awful, heart-in-your-mouth ticking was meant to stop once the hour of solving and escaping was up. Generally, at this point the players had completed the task already and I had thrown the doors wide for them, but in the unlikely event that they'd failed to escape by then I was meant to press another button and some relaxing muzak-y jazz started up to bring everyone's heart rates down. This allowed everyone a chance to look sheepishly at one another and pretend that the shame of not escaping wouldn't dog them for the rest of their lives. I then liberated them back into the world, shamefaced and changed.

As I stopped the ticking with a squeeze of my hand, I watched this group of players relax at their change of circumstance. Relief: the game was over, even if they'd won nothing. Usually, the ones that failed to escape made the same array of noises: wheezes of recrimination, gruff but well-meaning allotting of blame, and small laughs to show that the humiliation would only be temporary. In all the months I'd had this job as an attendant, employed to stand in the shadows in my toga with my papier-mâché helmet and mask, I had to say it was rare that anyone failed. An hour *should* have been ample time to get out of this escape room. The tasks that the participants had to complete were not without their challenges, sure – what would be the fun in that? – but I wouldn't have called them exacting or arduous; an hour to complete the room's puzzles and riddles should have been plenty. True, this lot were the day's final party and by this stage of the evening it was always likely everyone would be fairly wasted before they even stepped through the door into my dark. Drink tended to slow everything down. The owner of this escape room, Max, tried to maintain a strict but practicably unenforceable no-alcohol policy for the space, but I was hardly about to frisk anybody as they stepped over the boundary into the room, or break character to ask why a contestant's bottle of Evian smelled like off-brand Smirnoff Ice.

This current group of failures were waiting for the lights to come up. I wouldn't say patiently, but at that point politely. They were impatient to relax. They wanted to slink back into the foyer, victorious, ready to have their photo taken with the 'WE DID NOT GET OUT' sign we have above the till.

The group looked to me, the only attendant.

I did not move.

One of their number approached – a tall man, or holding himself so that he was taller than me, at least. He couldn't see well in the dark and extended a hand as if to try touching my chest. I could tell that he wondered, just for a second, whether I was a mannequin.

'So!' he said, brightly. 'We suck!'

I stared straight ahead. I was in character.

'What happens now?' he asked.

I continued to stare straight ahead. I was in character, and waiting to see if he was too.

The design of the room was not fiendish. Last season it had been Alice in Wonderland-themed, and I was dressed as a caterpillar. This month, however, it was loosely based on the Minotaur's labyrinth, and I was meant to be a quasi-Theseus figure. What that made the contestants, exactly, I wasn't sure: I was hazy about the myth apart from the fact that Max thought it wasn't going to fall foul of any copyright laws. Max hadn't adapted the layout of the escape room at all, or any of the puzzles, apart from the addition of a forking path through it made from cheap plywood partitions painted black. It would have been very underwhelming as a set, really, if seen in the full glare of light. Max had ensured that the windows had been fully blacked out and the internal light source was only low, pulsing, purple and at calf level. This design choice meant that visitors to the room were unable to easily discern its dimensions and size, supplying extra tension as they tried to solve the puzzles and get out. Add to this the judicious use of dry ice, and the participants' vision was obscured, a little candyfloss-clouded, and the air almost pearly and viscous around them as they bellowed instructions at each other or scrabbled at the props dotted about. I'd heard that some of our competitors' businesses made use of multiple rooms or huge complex spaces with many levels. Ours really was just a single space. I believed the building had once been a video store that Max was able to rent cheaply. He'd sourced all the props, come up with the gimmicks and slapdash paint-work. It was quite the money-spinner, all things told. My salary was one of the few expenses, and people paid well for this type of thing.

The players huddled together.

'Is this part of it?' a confident voice called out. 'Part of the puzzle?'

When I'd first taken this job, answering the advert Max had put up in the local newsagent's window, I'd taken some pleasure in both the concept of an escape room and my role in it. It could be interesting to watch how a sealed room either brought people together or rent them apart. Birthdays, stag dos. Take an example from just this morning: I presided over a group comprising various office colleagues who raced through their hour booking as part of a scheduled 'team-building away day'. The woman I understood to be the boss immediately began delegating roles while another in their cohort began quietly but audibly running a commentary on how everyone was contributing while his peers set about the business of escaping. They were efficient and joyless: it was team-building with sepulchral verve.

The room's next visitors were a family of five looking to flee the rain outside, choosing abject frustration and captivity to while away their lunchtime. I watched them hunch over the Gordian knots of oversized combination padlocks and count on their fingers as they mouthed clues like, 'My first is in butter, but never aloud', to begin with in wonder for comic effect and then ramping, genuine exasperation. They asked me for a hint to one riddle, and as I duly supplied by pointing a finger at a painted tile on the wall, I was close enough to watch the dopamine swell their pupils.

I had played host to six groups already before this final troop came through the doors. Any fascination I might have had in the first couple of groups had now passed through boredom and into something more livid, more galling.

How dare they fail, something said in my blood. *All trying to have a chance to be a hero.*

The tall man was replaced in my line of vision by a woman. She had little earrings in the shape of Christmas puddings. They were not in keeping with Max's hoped-for Minotaur and labyrinth aesthetic.

'Phewph!' she said.

'Well then,' she said.

'Can you—' she began, then she bobbed a little apologetically on the balls of her feet and returned to the group. They surrounded her as a herd might one of their wounded young if close to a predator. Her feet were loud as she stepped; everything seemed loud now, without the ticking. The ticking I'd had to put up with all day.

'We only paid for an hour,' one of the group said. I didn't catch who it was, and it scarcely mattered. I maintained my dignified silence, my stolid stance.

I'd noticed the demographic of players who booked parties here tended mostly to be students, overexcited stag dos and overworked young professionals. But of course – if your lives were full of stress and constraint, why not relax by putting yourself through an entirely fictitious new source of frustration. *What are you escaping?* I wanted to ask in my early months in the job as I watched the players toil away, seeking the fulfilment of release or lapping up the humiliation of failure. It must for some of them have been about the appeal of being in a group, as much as the satisfaction of problem-solving. Many types of people clearly thought that this type of shared intensity, this kind of communal act of throwing off a frenzied, self-induced claustrophobia was bonding in some way. The idea of facing something formidable, together, where you could prove your mettle to people that mattered to you. It was nice to see people on the brink of a breakthrough, of course, and to allow real life to be suspended even if just for an hour. I was part of that: just more set-dressing in my papier-mâché helmet hanging over my eyes, looming out of the dark.

I could see the attraction of extracting yourself from the world, certainly. Like that stage of a yawn when you went completely deaf, there was a feeling of respite before a fear set in that it might be forever.

I thought, I would only enjoy that feeling if I could also be alone. An escape room for one seems a far better notion. A butterfly in its cocoon.

One of the group tapped his smartwatch, its sudden blue light a beacon in the murk of the maze.

'Come on, pal,' he said, coming right up to me, squinting as if he could ever find my eyes in this light, beneath this mask.

'Go on Richard, move him out of the way,' his colleague muttered behind him. 'Bloody out-of-work actor.'

It had been too long a day in the labyrinth for that. I'd been rehearsing my backstory for days, that infernal ticking beating out a rhythm. Seven solid hours on my feet watching people spend money to have problems. They wanted a Minotaur, they brought their china shop to my bull, and talked to me like that? I could laugh in their faces, frothing in the corners of my cudhot mouth, while ensuring they never found their way out. You pulled my chain, the thread of me, and I'd show you nail marks on the walls, etched along in parallel lines at hip level. You'd have no idea whether they'd been caused by someone coming or going; nail marks that looked like musical staves, as if anyone would make up songs about how hard you'd battled, how hard this had all been for you.

I could keep up my *attendance* all day, you trivial little man.

I did not say any of this, but I did meet his eye. He looked on the verge of tears.

I had always been good at standing still. For a while, I made my money as a life model at different art schools, and then for a spate I worked as a living statue. I made a kind of approximation of the Tin Man out of foil and body paint. I found I was well liked by passers-by, and my hat had a steady stream of coins. I even went to a convention once. Can you imagine! The whole town full of static, uncanny figures vying for attention. I kept cuttings of it in a scrapbook I kept in my car; I was sleeping there at the time as I am now, my wife having left me and taken the house. All the predictable puns made it into the local press about the novel convention – 'Stiff Competition! A Solid Line-Up!' But what I recalled most vividly about the trip was not the days spent standing in the street performing, but rather the evenings. All the performers let down their hair, untableauing their vivants by the local hotel bar and massaging life back into their shoulders and aching shins. Most of the performers didn't bother removing their costumes before taking to the dance floor. It was obvious that the living statues' finery was not designed for movement. The clank of plastic and tinfoil breast-plates thudded softer, ungainly beats beneath the music. Mimes showed shocking red tongues to the ceiling as they chanted lyrics to each other, trying out their voices for the first time in hours.

I remembered how across the cheap hotel ballroom, naked bands of skin flashed at wrists and ankles as sleeves were tugged over elbows, robes were pulled high. It was an evening of makeup thumbed from earlobes and the corners of eyes: it must have been hell for the cleaners the morning after.

Standing in the corner, still shy and agog, I remember watching body paint falling away in flakes and crusts and puffs and motes, the air of the bar growing silty with their movement. False masonry and fake lichen floated down to my feet, my Tin Man Midas-pelt catching the disco lights.

'Please,' said one of the players in the smallest voice.

A sudden crick in my neck and I turned my chin a little, not wanting them to see my smile.

Acknowledgements

Severe gale force 9 imminent. Sincere thanks to all at 4th Estate, especially steadfast captain Kishani Widyaratna. Thank you Katy Archer and Eliza Plowden, and Nicole Jashapara, Lottie Fyfe and Amber Burlinson – sorry for the [*sic*].

Squalls. Thanks as ever to Lucy Luck for being stern and delighting at all the right moments. Thank you, Saida Azizova.

Rough or very rough, becoming moderate or rough later. Versions of some of these stories benefited from initial individual publication and commission, and I am indebted to their editors' care and attentiveness. Thank you to anyone making hard-won time and deep space for short fiction. Emma Warnock at No Alibis Press! Sarah Cleave at Comma Press! Claire Shanahan and all those involved with the NSSA! Nathaniel Kunitsky at Knight Errant Press! 3 of Cups Press' Clare Bogen, Anna Coatman and Alice Slater! Gerónimo Sarmiento

Cruz at the *Chicago Review*! *Praxis* editors Andrew Hodgson, Rosie Šnajdr and Chris Clarke! Nick Murray and their multivarious *Annexe*! Brodie Crellin and Luke Neima at *Granta*! Aoife Walsh at *The South Circular*! Mike Wendling and audio journal *4'33"*! Becky Ripley and her production team at BBC Radio! *The Junket*'s Kristen Treen, Jon Day and James Purdon! Emily Speed! Terry Craven! Tom Conaghan! S J Fowler and Enemies thereof! Declan Ryan and his Days of Roses! Jess Chandler at Prototype! Isabel Waidner for 8fold's *The Arrow Maker* and their anthology with Dostoyevsky Wannabe! Tim Etchells and Vlatka Horvat for their *Seen From Here* project supporting the Trussell Trust! Andrew Latimer at *Egress*! Heartfelt appreciation also to those who participated so generously during Influx Press' lockdown auction, donating to the Book Charity Hardship Fund – thank you Lauren, Michael C, K, Angela, Michael H, Matt, Bob, Burley Fisher, Chris, Gideon, Aki, CJW, Charlotte & Elizabeth & Grace, Tim, Sam, Alex, Terri-Jane, Sarah and Isabella. I have broken an online thesaurus trying to find *grateful* synonyms when it comes to Kit Caless and Gary Budden.

New low expected. David Collard and his increscent Carthorse Orchestra, and dear Nisha Ramayya & Špela Drnovšek Zorko – thank you for reminding me of better things and best things at tough times. Respect and thanks to colleagues and writers based at RHUL for their company, humour and talent over the years; thanks, UCU.

Backing southerly. This book would not have been possible without Jana Ondrejkovičová and her thoughtful, energising work, as well as Ann Leck and the Tuesday team for graceful wrangling, boundless cheer and peerless sausages. Thank you, Margaret and Richard Stevens, for your many kindnesses.

Rain or showers, fair later. Thank you for everything, Nell.